A MEASURE OF KNOWLEDGE

A MEASURE OF KNOWLEDGE (Justice #8)
ISBN-13 - 978-1-64918-024-7

Published by Angry Sheep Publishing
Findlay, Ohio

Cover Design by For the Muse Designs
Interior Design by JW Manus

A Measure of Knowledge

Justice #8

Suzan Harden

Justice
(the novels)

Justice: The Beginning
A Question of Balance
A Modicum of Truth
A Matter of Death
A Touch of Mother
A Twist of Love
A Virtue of Child
A Hand of Father
A Measure of Knowledge
A Hint of Thief

The Justice Thalia Stories
Snowfall

Murder Most Fowl

The Sweetest Poison

A Granddaughter of Mine

More Stories
Sword and Sorceress 28 ("Justice")
Sword and Sorceress 30 ("Diplomacy in the Dark")

Tales of the Twelve
The Trickster Priestess and the Demon

For updates, news, and giveaways, join Suzan's mailing list or visit her website at www.suzanharden.com. You can also check her out on Twitter @Suzan_Harden or on Facebook at SuzanHardenWriter.

Prologue

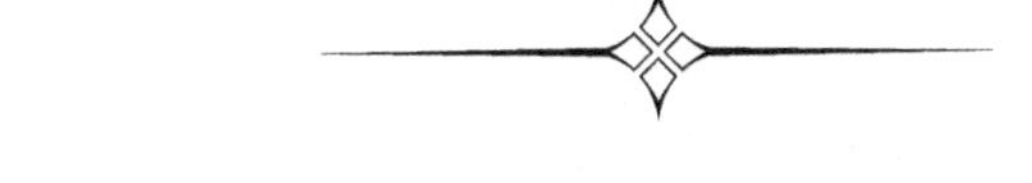

One sunny day, Knowledge sat in her library, cataloguing all the animals and plants for Child. Balance had created so many Child feared She would forget one of them. If She did, and that creature or plant died alone, the World would be a poorer place for the loss.

Knowledge's brother Thief burst through her door. "Sister! Sister! Come quick! I found an unknown creature!"

"There's no such thing as an unknown creature," Knowledge retorted. "Now, go amuse Yourself with one of the Others. I am busy creating a list of all living things for Child."

"Then You should be able to identify the creature I found." Thief tugged on Her sleeve. "Come with Me. Please!"

Knowledge set aside Her quill and glared at Her brother. "You will pester Me until I come with You, won't You?"

"Of course," He said with a cheeky grin.

"I will fetch Child," Knowledge said. "She will want to see this new creature, too."

When They approached Child in her garden, She quickly agreed to join Her Brother and Sister. "Are You sure this creature is not an ill bear or wolf?"

Thief shrugged. "I did not recognize it which was why I came to Knowledge."

Knowledge and Child followed Thief deep into the forest. Knowledge questioned whether Thief was playing tricks on Her again, something He delighted in doing.

They entered a thicket so dense the sun did not penetrate the leaves. However, the branches parted to allow the Three to make Their way to the center. They found Mother sitting on a blanket and nursing the creature. She greeted the Three and smiled. "Come see Your new Brother."

"Brother?" Child laughed and clapped Her hands. "This is wonderful news, Mother."

"But . . . It doesn't look like Us." Knowledge cocked her head. "It looks more like the first creatures Balance created."

"And It was alone when I first saw It." Thief frowned.

"I was thirsty and hungry after birthing Him," Mother said. "He is one of Us, so no animal or plant would dare to try to harm Him."

Knowledge reached forward and petted Her new brother's fur. It was softer than the finest rabbit's. But as she touched Him, He wiggled and shifted until His fur and limbs were gone, and scales covered Him instead.

Thief laughed at His brother's change. "Can He become anything, even some creature Balance never thought of?"

As if in answer, the Babe shifted again. The scales faded, and sharp quills covered Him. Yet, He nursed contentedly from Mother's bosom.

"He needs a name," Knowledge said.

"What would You call Him?" Child asked. "If We put together every creature He morphs into, that would be a very long name indeed."

"I would call him Wildling," Knowledge said with a firm nod of her head. "So far He has only become the animals of the forests and mountains and plains, but not any of the animals You have given to humans."

"I like that," Child said. "May I give Him the wild animals of the forest and mountains and plains as His birth gift, Mother?"

"That is very generous of You, Child." Mother smiled. "He will be pleased with such a gift."

"And I can show Him all the hidden places of the World," Thief said.

Knowledge carefully stroked Wildling's quills. "Would You show Me the form You wore when Thief first saw You?"

The Babe drew away from Mother's breast. He wiggled and shifted again until He was in the rough form of Father except Wildling was covered in thick, luxurious brown hair all over His body not just His head. His big brown eyes gazed at Thief.

"I like this Sibling." Thief nodded. "We can share much."

"Mother, may I make a creature that resembles Wildling?" Child asked. "Like I made people?"

"That is up to Him," Mother replied.

Wildling nodded. So Child created beings in Wildling's true form. Like Wilding Himself, they preferred the mountains and forests.

Knowledge thought long and hard about what to call these new beings. Hairy Men was the best she could do since it accurately described the new beings.

However, the humans were not happy about their new cousins. They feared the Hairy Men's relationship with the wild predators who would eat people if they could. To protect the Hairy Men, Wildling and Thief taught them how to hide in the most inaccessible areas of the World.

Eventually, the Hairy Men faded into the people's dim legends. But every once in a while hunters, lumberers, and miners come across large footprints. And even rarer, they hear the Hairy Men's lonely cries at night.

— The Twenty-Fifth Book of Knowledge, Verses I thru XXIV

Chapter 1

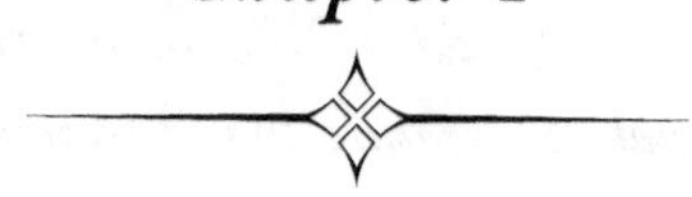

Chill rains had settled over the city of Orrin after the Winter Solstice, and everyone who didn't have to be out in the drizzles and downpours stayed close to their fireplaces and braziers. Those same storms had halted ship traffic in and out of our harbor, and the fierce waves made it too dangerous for the fishers to launch their smaller boats. That left repairs and crafts to occupy idle hands until the weather broke.

I found myself with four justices in residence where there had only been me at Orrin's Temple of Balance last winter. Justice Erato and Brother Wolf Run, who currently rode circuit in the east side of the Duchy of Orrin, had come to my Temple to resupply in the late fall, but early and deep snows in the foothills forced them to retreat and spend the season here rather than Mountain Gate as they'd planned.

However, our visitors were not bored. The bonding of the city's clergy over the difficulties of the last year had led to spending our free time together on the long, dark nights. Each Temple took turns hosting games, story telling, and music except on Rest Day. We'd gather after First Evening, and a competition of a different sort had broken out among our head cooks and chefs over the quality and variety of dishes served.

On this Sixth Day of the week of Midwinter, we were gathered in the sanctuary of the Temple of Thief for a Mill tournament. Quite simply, wagering on games of skill and chance was His domain. Therefore, there was never any question that a great deal of betting would occur any time we assembled at Thief.

The spiced roasts of beef and venison filled the air of the Temple with a hearty aroma. Dried cranberries imported from the eastern side of the Northern Long Continent flavored the extravagantly expensive wheat bread. Turnips and potatoes were boiled and mashed together before butter, milk, and black pepper were added. Instead of Pana Valley wine, Thief's cook served a Kemet-style beer from an inn in Nastine. The yeasty drink complimented the meat and vegetables' savory taste.

Since the Temple of Thief did not have an eternal flame before the statue of the god they represented, the architects compensated by building two large fireplaces on the northern and southern walls of their main sanctuary. Oil lamps with reflectors hung from the ceiling. Unfortunately, they all made a vast amount of heat, which meant I spent most of the night squinting against their uncomfortable pink glares. Only the obsidian statue of Thief Himself remained cool enough not to bother my odd eyesight.

My head of household Sivan watched Baby Kosumi so my junior justice Yanaba could attend the festivities. I rather suspected it was my assistant's way of suggesting she and my chief warden make their relationship more permanent with a babe of their own.

The pleasant thing about Mill was everyone from Balance could play, too. Talbert made a point of creating game pieces of two different types of material so my sister justices could study the board by touch.

I was the odd one, a justice who had vision, though my perception was different from other sighted humans. I perceived differences due to relative heat exuded by the things, people, and animals around me. Therefore, I could actually see the game set and the pieces clearly.

"Your move, Anthea." Sister Cedar Grove smirked at me from across our table.

That was the other thing I loved about our gatherings. We agreed to drop all titles for the duration of our entertainments. It was freeing not to have to worry about etiquette and status for a few candlemarks.

It also helped that none of us wore Temple robes to these gatherings. Cedar Grove wore a skirt and a loose tunic to keep her growing belly warm. I wore a velvet dress, also for warmth and not fashion. The garment had been made by an Orrin seamstress named Jaci. She wanted to gift it to me for saving her family from being eaten by two wechuges. I insisted on paying for the dress. In the end, we agreed I would pay for the material and thread, and Jaci could spend her free time as she wished.

"I am aware, thank you, Cedar Grove." I growled as I stared at the board. Mill was less complicated than chess, but it still required a certain amount of strategy. It didn't help that this was the last game. As the two finalists, Cedar Grove and I were tied at two games apiece. The winner would take the tournament and the prize gold.

As I said before, no games could be played at Thief without some gambling involved.

The staff of Thief paused in their removal of empty dishes from the serving table and watched the game. The crowd of clergy pressed closer and murmured among themselves. Secondary betting among the clergy, staff, and wardens impinged on my awareness. I saw the trap Cedar Grove was about to spring. The question was finding a way out.

Or maybe I was looking at the problem from the wrong perspective. Maybe I needed to go around. I slid the copper peg into the hole.

Cedar Grove's breath came out in a *whoosh*.

"Are you all right, my love?" Garbhan's hand was on her shoulder.

She frowned at the board, trying to figure out my plan. Both of her palms rubbed her swollen belly. "I would be if our daughter would stop kicking my lungs."

"Do you concede?" I smirked at her.

She snorted. "To you? Never!" Still, the Thief priestess took her time, which set off another round of wagering among our peers. She took the space I'd expected, and I made my next move.

Her face fell. She had only two moves left. One where she would lose the match and one where she would tie. Cedar Grove had too much pride to deliberately lose.

So did I.

Pandemonium exploded as we inserted our last pegs into their squares. No one was expecting us to tie. The brothers and sisters of Thief were laughing as they took the gambling proceeds to the dais on which the statue of Thief stood in order to count them.

Cedar Grove and I stood and bowed to each other. I stretched my arms over my head and arched my back to pull out the knots. Garbhan guided her over to the food table. He'd become rather overprotective of the priestess since he'd seeded her womb. I was sure it was difficult not to form an attachment when bringing a new life into the world.

My thoughts dragged my attention to Luc, the High Brother of Light. He stood next to the seat of Thief Talbert, and they both grinned like fools. I realized why. After the Temple of Thief took its cut and the prize gold was split between Cedar Grove and me, the remaining coins were being divided between the two high brothers.

I stalked over to them. "What is going on here?"

"Collecting on our bets," Luc said innocently.

"Y-you bet I would lose?" I'd never thought of myself as being that egotistic, but his judgement of my skill hurt.

He leaned on his left crutch and cupped my cheek. "I know you. And I knew you wouldn't lose."

Confusion rippled through me. "B-but—"

"Balance in all things, Anthea," Talbert teased. "You of all people should know that."

"You bet that we would tie?" I shook my head at their foolishness. Or wisdom, depending on one's point of view. "You two are—"

"Brilliant?" Luc offered.

"Ingenious?" Talbert said.

"Pains in my backside," I retorted.

Shi Hua's screams interrupted our byplay. Jeremy cradled the Light priestess as she collapsed to the marble floor of the sanctuary.

I raced over, knelt next to Shi Hua, and tried to absorb her pain. Fire ripped through my belly as if sharp claws had gutted me. *Breathe with me, Shi Hua. What's wrong?*

It took several moments for the young woman's agony to recede. At first, I feared a complication from childbirth though she'd delivered little Chao nearly four weeks ago. But it wasn't her pain I was feeling. It was someone else's. Someone who couldn't see her attacker. Someone who had either passed out or died from her injuries. But before she did, I felt the distinctive rasp of demon magic.

"Mei Wen!" Shi Hua gasped between her words and tears. "She tried to—tried to warn me. A demon army has invaded Chengzhou."

Chapter 2

This was one of those times when I truly would have traded all my other gifts granted by the Twelve for the ability to distance speak in order to know what was happening in Jing. Together, Jeremy and I helped Shi Hua upright and to a chair.

High Mother Leocadia brought a cup of water for the distraught Light priestess. "Should we summon a healer?"

"No, and shield your thoughts. All of you," Shi Hua snapped. "I need some breathing room."

It wasn't like the Jing woman to lose her temper, but only then did I realize how close our fellow clergy were crowding around us. The energy of their worry for her and concern about Justice Mei Wen's warning was enough to set my own teeth on edge.

"You heard Sister Shi Hua," High Brother Talbert said. "Everyone take a chair or a bench while we sort this out."

Murmurs filled the room. With the mention of demons, unease filtered past many minds despite Shi Hua's pointed request for the clergy to shield their thoughts. But everyone did as Talbert asked except for the twelve Temple seats and Brother Jeremy. He fed his own energy into Shi Hua.

The rapid crimson throb of the blood vessels in her neck slowly dulled to her natural orangish-red hue now she was no longer subjected to Justice Mei Wen's pain. However, she continued to rub her abdomen.

"Anthea, you should sit down, too." Talbert pulled a second chair closer to Shi Hua. "We don't need you passing out either."

High Brother Han of Conflict firmly grasped my left elbow and shuffled me to the second chair. I had the impression he would have picked me up as one would a recalcitrant child if I had refused. Truth be told, my own knees were shaky from the intensity of the link with Shi Hua's friend.

Once seated, I said, "Justice Mei Wen was definitely attacked by a demon."

Talbert folded his arms over his chest. "Is she still alive?"

I looked at Shi Hua.

"I don't know," she murmured. Hot, red drops trickled down her cheeks.

"Who else can we contact in Chengzhou for confirmation of the attack?" I asked.

"Are you saying she lied?" Fury reddened Shi Hua's skin to the point I could no longer see her tears.

"No, I'm terrified she's dead, and we may have just lost Jing." I looked up at Talbert. "Could you please send someone to the Jing embassy? Ambassador Quan should be informed."

He turned and barked the order to his chief warden, Sabine. As I expected, she exited to the rear of the sanctuary. A horse would be much quicker, and Sabine was smart enough to take another warden or three with her to the embassy district. The Jing guards would take a squad of Temple wardens more seriously than a single messenger.

I took Shi Hua's left hand in both of my own. "What about Reverend Father Biming?"

She shook head and wiped her cheeks with her free hand. "We weren't supposed to speak until Third Evening on First Day. Things have been so quiet lately with the fierce winter across the Northern Hemisphere—"

"That may be exactly what the demons were waiting for," Han said.

"Are you saying we've been lackadaisical?" High Brother Jax of Wildling snapped.

"No," High Sister Mya of Child said. She stood very close to Talbert, their robes touching, which allowed him to shield her with his quicksilver talents. It said how bad the emotions and thoughts were leaking from the junior clergy. No wonder Shi Hua lost her temper earlier.

"It's simply human nature to relax when a supposed threat doesn't materialize," Mya continued. "Not even the creatures of the forests and mountains can maintain such vigilance indefinitely."

"Neither the emperor or the Temple heads in Jing would simply let a demon army enter the capital," Shi Hua said angrily.

"No one is saying they would," Brother Jeremy murmured soothingly. "Everyone is upset, and they shouldn't conjecture the status of Chengzhou before we have more information." He looked up and glared at everyone surrounding the mother of his child.

"It's better Shi Hua's doesn't try right now anyway," Luc said. "If she were to do so, it could split the attention of the person while they are fighting for their life."

"And that may be the critical moment where the tide of the battle is turned," I added.

"So, what would you have us do, Anthea?" High Sister Mariana of Knowledge glared at me. "Nothing?"

Mariana and I were barely civil to each other after I called her out for shirking her duties last summer. She wasn't a renegade or evil per se, just lazy and self-centered. And her laziness and self-centered behavior had cost lives in Orrin.

I bit my tongue before I said any of the thoughts about her racing through my mind. "No, But I'm not putting Sister Shi Hua's sanity or life at risk until we consult with Ambassador Quan. He was gracious enough to petition the Jing Temple of Light on our behalf to allow

Sister Shi Hua to supplement our own Temple of Light after we lost so many of our own brothers to the renegades. I don't wish to throw away either her life or our diplomatic relationship with Jing out of fear."

My answer was obviously not the one Mariana was expecting from the way she shrunk back at my withering logic. She met the eyes of each of our fellow seats, but she found no support.

Jeremy looked up at Luc from where the younger priest crouched next to Shi Hua. "Why don't Garbhan and I take the sister back to our Temple for some rest?"

"No," Shi Hua spat. "Chief Warden Sabine will bring the ambassador here, so I will wait for him. Here."

Even I was taken aback by Shi Hua's blatant insubordination. This behavior was not like her at all, which meant the short contact with Justice Mei Wen had shaken her far more than I'd realized.

Thank Balance, Cedar Grove approached our little group before Luc could open his mouth to reprimand the young Light priestess. "Shi Hua, would you please accompany me to my chambers while we wait for the ambassador? I have some private questions for you if you don't mind." She made a point of patting her own growing belly.

The Thief priestess's attempted distraction didn't fool anyone, but Shi Hua pushed to her feet. She pointedly looked at Jeremy and said, "I'd be glad to answer your questions concerning my experience birthing a child. Alone."

Cedar Grove shot a look at Garbhan and shook her head. Both priests had the appearance of dejected suitors, which in a way, they were. The two women headed toward the doorway leading to the Thief clergy's private rooms.

"What did I do?" Garbhan whined.

"You had the misfortune of being blessed with a penis," I said.

A few of the people around us did a poor job of hiding their snickers.

"Anthea." There was a warning in Luc's voice. "You are not helping matters."

"Someone had to lighten the mood." I sighed and took the cup High Brother Xander of Death handed to me. The sweet taste of Pana red wine took the edge off my own nerves. "The rest of you didn't feel what happened to Justice Mei Wen."

"What did happen, Anthea?" High Brother Jax asked.

I closed my eyes and concentrated on the memory of the link. "The Jing justice is blind—"

"As a proper justice should be," High Father Jerrod of Father scoffed.

I ignored his nasty comment and continued, "—so I have no visual clues. The Temple bells were ringing the demon alarm code." I focused on the tolling Mei Wen heard, trying to identify each Temple. "Balance. Conflict. Mother, Father, Light."

My limbs trembled as my mind replayed the slight, but intense, contact. "The Reverend Mother of Balance is shouting orders. Steel against stone. Cries of pain. Mei Wen's own warden is cut down. She slips and lands on marble flooring. Warm, sticky, copper-tasting. It's her warden's blood. Another human is dragging her away from the fighting. The rancid taste of demon magic. Fire across her belly—"

At the intense pain, my eyes flew open. I half-expected to see my own entrails spilling into my lap.

"It's all right, Anthea." Luc's warm grip on my hands was far more reassuring than his words. "You're here with me in Orrin."

I gulped air. My face was wet from the other justice's pain. "It feels like it was a concerted attack on all twelve of the home Temples in Chengzhou. The Justice wasn't in contact with Shi Hua long enough for the alarms to cycle through, but if five were ringing at the same time—"

"It's best to assume the demons struck all twelve at the same time," Talbert said.

"Separate the imperial forces from the Temples, and the Temples from each other." Han nodded. "Sound strategy."

"What about Jing's philosophical schools?" Leocadia folded her hands inside the sleeves of her robes, probably so the rest of the clergy couldn't see them shaking. "Surely, they would aid both the emperor and the Temples."

"Emperor Bao Chengwu executed any member of the School of Sorcery he could find after they sided with the renegades," Luc said darkly. "While all the schools deal with talent to some extent, I doubt the emperor has much faith in any of them, especially since his own father was a member of the School of Sorcery.

"You are correct in that regard, High Brother," a familiar voice rang out behind me.

I turned to find Ambassador Quan striding into the sanctuary of Thief. He was accompanied by four of his own guards and his alleged concubine Yin Li, as well as the wardens led by Sabine.

"Our emperor only keeps his own father alive out of paternal courtesy." Quan approached me and cocked his head. "What trouble have you stirred up this time, my dear Chief Justice?"

Chapter 3

Talbert magically amplified his voice. "All junior clergy are to return to your Temples immediately."

There was a great deal of grumbling among our subordinates, but I understood their resentment of being left out during major discussions. Elizabeth, the former chief justice of Tandor and the soon-to-be chief justice of the newly formed Duchy of Anacapa, whispered to Yanaba and Erato.

I stood and added, "Your seats will inform you of our additional findings. But considering this is a foreign ally, please allow us the discretion of diplomacy before you all get your hackles up over being excluded."

Most of the clergy weren't sure whether to be insulted until my justices and half of the Wildlings laughed. That seemed to ease everyone else's minds.

Quan approached me. "Findings?"

I lowered my voice. "Let the sanctuary clear first. Then, we'll explain everything."

It took nearly a quarter of a candlemark for the visiting clergy and their wardens to gather and don winter cloaks. At the same time, Thief's staff cleared tables and brought in steaming pots of black Jing and Meca bean teas.

Yin Li stayed as well on the pretense of the ambassador's trusted advisor. She wasn't simply an Imperial concubine. Known to only a few in the room, Yin Li was a priestess of Love, Quan's personal bodyguard, and Shi Hua's aunt. As fierce of a fighter as the Love priestess was, I knew I never wanted to face Yin Li in battle, but I'd definitely want her on my side.

The chief wardens who had not attended this evening's entertainment were alerted. Since Elizabeth remained at our impromptu convocation as a courtesy to a visiting seat, my own chief warden Little Bear brought his second Gina. She had accepted Elizabeth's offer to become her chief warden when she moved to the islands this spring, so it only made sense for Gina to assume some of those responsibilities.

There had been a time when all wardens had been excluded from a convocation of the Temple seats. However, with the spate of demon attacks over the course of the last year and a half, it seemed unwise not to include those who were responsible for Temple security. Knowledge was essential to preparedness as Little Bear constantly pointed out to me.

Once Cedar Grove and Shi Hua returned to the Thief's sanctuary and the household staff departed, Talbot warded the huge room. I sat with the statue of Thief to my back and pulled my hood as forward as I could to keep from squinting at the heat from the fires.

Han took the seat to my left and muttered, "You should have been in Conflict, Anthea."

"Why is that?" I asked softly.

"You're the only one besides me, Jax, and Talbert who keeps their back covered and sits where they can keep an eye on the doors and windows."

I chuckled. "I'm afraid that's sheer experience, my friend."

It could have been worse. Elizabeth sat between Leocadia and Mya because she still had problems being around men after the tortures the skinwalkers who had taken over Tandor had put her through for a year. I couldn't imagine being so damaged I couldn't sit between Han and Quan as I did now.

Shi Hua and I related each of our impressions during the brief contact with Justice Mei Wen. Cedar Grove had blocked the emotional response from Mei Wen, and Shi Hua was able to recall a little more than I had. Flashbangs detonated in the streets. The amplified voices of officers of the imperial armies giving orders. The *whoosh* of thousands of arrows launched at the same moment.

Quan took the news without comment. He wore a solemn mien as he played with the gold beads that decorated the ends of his long moustache. Finally, he exhaled and said, "I believe Brother Jian of Light is our backup if we cannot contact Reverend Father Biming at Third Evening local time."

"And Brother Fa after him." Shi Hua sounded so damn tired. I could understand why. Exhaustion tugged at my eyelids, and I didn't have nearly the contact with Justice Mei Wen that Shi Hua did.

"Are they both in Chengwu?" Luc asked.

Shi Hua shook her head. "No." She glanced at the ambassador, but he showed no reaction, so her attention returned to Luc. "When I was assigned to the ambassador, Reverend Father Biming made sure my additional contacts were in three different Temples and assigned to three different cities. Justice Mei Wen was appointed as the emperor's legal advisor five years ago, which is why she is also in Chengzou.

"It's the middle of winter." High Brother Ben of Vintner rubbed his chin. "With this year's storms, we may not get conventional word until next spring."

Han snorted. "It was a year before we learned of the takeover of our own sister city of Tandor. What makes you think we'll learn what happened in Chengzou before a demon army sails into our harbor?"

Leave it to the high brother of Conflict to give voice to my own fears.

I cleared my throat. "If all else fails, Sister Shi Hua, would you be able to contact your mother?"

She looked at me uncertainly. "I could, but she's a farmer."

"Certainly there's a Temple in your home village?" Leave it to Luc to ascertain where I was going with my questions.

"Of course, but—"

"This may be the advantage of me learning the Jing language," I said. "If the ambassador, High Brother Luc, and I join the link with you, your mother, and the priest or priestess she trusts in your village—"

"We could tax her abilities," Quan protested.

"She's stronger than you give her credit for," I retorted.

"She just gave birth." Quan glared at me.

"Four weeks ago," Shi Hua snapped as she abruptly stood. "I'm fully healed."

Cedar Grove rose, too, laid a hand on Shi Hua's shoulder, and whispered in the Jing priestess's ear. Slowly, both women sat again, though Shi Hua gave the ambassador a rather murderous look.

"Anthea and I can boost Shi Hua's resources," Luc said. "And you're the highest ranking Jing official we have to prove our identities."

Yin Li cleared her throat. "With all due respect to you, Ambassador, and you, High Brother, it might be better if I participate instead. I personally know the Love sisters in Yintze."

"All of this is moot if we can contact Reverend Father Biming tonight." Talbert sat with his elbows on his knees and his hands clasped together. The pose showed just how worried he was.

But then, so was I.

"Let's take this one step at a time," I said. "We'll try to contact Reverend Father Biming tonight. If we can't, then we send messages concerning the situation to Queen Teodora, the Matriarch of the Diné, and the King of Cant at first morning. They can alert their own distance speakers and triangulate until we get an answer from Chengzhou."

Surprisingly, the other Temple seats agreed to my idea. They also agreed to retreat to their own Temples with my promise to give them an answer about whether tonight's efforts were successful or not. In turn, I asked them to pray to their own deities for our success.

When they left, Quan looked at me and shook his head. "I never thought I'd see you ask your colleagues to pray for their own patrons of the Twelve to intercede on your behalf."

I chuckled as I donned my winter cloak. "I hope the other Eleven take pity on me. I know damn well Balance won't answer my prayers."

Chapter 4

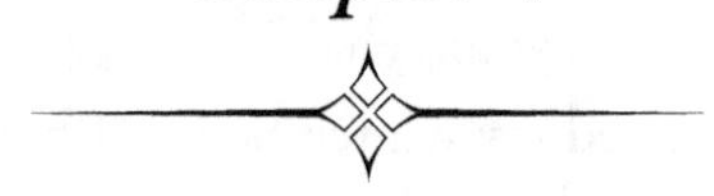

We retreated to the Temple of Light so Shi Hua had a chance to rest in her own bed before we attempted to contact Biming. I sent Gina and Elizabeth back to Balance along with my winnings from tonight's Mill tournament.

My fellow justice joked she would keep the bag of money. To which, her future chief warden threatened to resign because she couldn't work with a dishonest justice. Neither of them realized I planned to buy farewell gifts for both of them before they left Orrin. In fact, I'd already placed the orders with the smiths under contract with our Temple.

As for the rest of my winnings, I just hoped I'd live long enough to figure out what to do with the money. I was so used to the order of Balance taking care of my immediate needs. It hadn't occurred to me to spend anything. Well, beyond my basic stipend with which I bought treats on Bakers Street.

Balance help me, I hadn't even been able to do that for the past year. Not with the rash of attempts on my life since I was sentenced to the Balance seat of Orrin. My chief warden put his foot down when it came to me even thinking about leaving Balance without an escort. With the closing of the tunnels beneath Orrin, I couldn't even sneak out any more.

Meanwhile, the ambassador had a lively . . . discussion with Sisters Yin Li and Shi Hua in their own language I made an effort to ignore until I heard my name. Quan finally took Shi Hua's side and sent Yin Li back to the embassy with the suggestion her son Yin Shang needed her more than Shi Hua did. Yin Li was obviously not happy about his decision, but she bowed deeply before she mounted her horse and left with two of the Jing guards.

While Shi Hua retreated to her bedchamber, Talbert, Ambassador Quan, and I joined Luc in his private dining room. Neither the Jing guards nor our wardens were pleased about being excluded in this discussion, but after tonight's events, I needed a break from their constant worry rubbing against my mental shields. It was worse than a poorly fitted boot chaffing my heel.

"Po?" I said gently after I removed my cloak and gloves and took my chair. "Is there anything we can do for you?"

He blinked and looked at me from across the table. "I never had the chance to see my nephews." Out of everything he might have said, family sentiment would not have been my first guess.

"The layers of guards around the imperial palace—" Luc started.

"From what Shi Hua and Anthea describe, this attack was carefully planned." The ambassador waved his hand. "Maybe years in advance. Quick surgical knife strikes at all the Temple leadership at the same moment. It stands to reason those same targeted attacks hit at our guilds, our schools of philosophy, the nobility, and yes, even the imperial family."

He closed his eyes. An expression of sheer agony crossed his visage. "I never wanted the throne. Yet, my greatest fear may be coming true."

"We don't know what's happening exactly," I said.

"I don't want to be forced back home," Quan said. "Not this way."

"Sometimes, we have no choice in our duties," Luc murmured.

Before I could chide Luc for his insensitivity, his evening assistant Edberth entered with a tray. More Jing black tea from the scent. It was rapidly becoming the only thing to get me through my days. Or in this case, my nights.

Quan wasn't the only one who feared the news from his homeland. Until I knew the fate of my fellow justice, I would have difficulty sleeping. Nightmares of my own experiences with demons would make sure of that.

"We can plan based on the possible scenarios we face." Talbert met each of our gazes. "I'm not trying to be morbid. We can expect the best, but we must prepare for the worst."

Luc chuckled. "That should be your Temple's motto."

"The best case scenario is the Temples rally, and they and the schools work with the imperial army to deflect the invasion in Chengzhou." Quan murmured his thanks to Edberth when the former Light head of household handed the ambassador a cup of tea on a saucer.

"The worst case scenario is the Temple of Death triggered their last resort spells, and the nation of Jing no longer exists," I said bitterly.

"The Jing Temples of Balance and Death are aware of the techniques you and Chief Justice Elizabeth developed in Tandor, aren't they?" Edberth continued pouring tea as if we weren't talking about the potential destruction of the entire Old Continent. Thankfully, he didn't mention that our idea cost the lives of the surviving Tandoran Death clergy and our own High Sister Bertrice.

Luc looked as surprised at Edberth joining the conversation as I felt.

"Yes, they know," I said.

"Then trust them to protect the civilians as best they can." Edberth handed me a cup of tea. "It's no secret the rest of the world thinks the queens and Temples of Albion and Eire failed, but they saved as many of our ancestors as they could before they activated the last resort spells."

He continued pouring as if he were discussing the weather. "Not even the Jing clergy would do so without due consideration. I pray matters in your empire do not go so badly they must consider such a drastic course of action, Your Highness. Have faith Light and Knowledge will help them find a way to defeat the demons."

Those were the most words I'd ever heard Edberth speak at one time. Not even when he served my maternal grandfather Kam as head of household here at the Temple of Light had Edberth been so vocal.

"Wise words, Edberth." A ghost of a smile crossed Luc's face as he accepted his own cup of tea. "It's a pity you decided to cut back on your duties."

"It was time for Istaqa to take his place within the Temple, High Brother." Edberth inclined his head. "Shall I prepare any food for you and your guests, sir?" He made a point of looking at me.

I held up my left hand. "No, thank you. I am too worried to eat."

"What?" Quan mockingly exclaimed. "A day has come where the chief justice of Orrin's stomach is, dare I say it, full?"

"You didn't see the size of the bowl of mashed vegetables she ate at Thief earlier tonight," Talbert teased. "You're older now, Anthea. You keep eating the way you do, and you'll end up as round as Kam."

"My previous seat didn't exercise like his beloved granddaughter does," Edberth said. "You have nothing to fear, Chief Justice. And I believe we still have some almond pastries."

"Thank you, Edberth," I said graciously at his offer of my favorite treat. Istaqa's obsessive behavior as head of household was starting to make sense. However, there was no real reason to compare himself with Edberth. Nor did the former head of household interfere with Istaqa's duties. It was simply convenient to keep Edberth on staff in case Luc needed assistance in the middle of the night.

With a start, I realized this was the first time guilt didn't plague me over the loss of Luc's left foot.

Edberth smiled at me and left the dining room.

I waited until the door closed behind him before I glared at Talbert. "I may eat like Kam, but I don't drink wine by the barrel like he did."

"Which is a good thing," Luc said dryly. "The Orrin Light accounts show an excess for the first time in years, which is yet another reason Brother Garbhan was sent to spy on me."

I cocked my head. "Reverend Father Farrell is complaining because you're not spending enough on wine?"

"More like Lord Aleister is complaining his revenues are down, and the Pana Valley Temple of Vintner reported the losses to their home Temple," Talbot commented.

"I don't suppose Light could order extra barrels and trade them, could you?" I asked.

"I suppose I could give them to Talbert for gaming prizes if you would prefer wine to gold," Luc teased.

"I like the gold." I shook my head. "Besides, a portion of my winnings will go toward assisting Elizabeth in setting up the new Anacapa Temple of Balance."

"That should be the responsibility of your home Temple." Quan frowned. "Surely, your Reverend Mother doesn't expect you and the Orrin Temple to provide the supplies and coin—"

I held up both hands. "Calm down, Ambassador. I'm using it for gifts I was planning to purchase for Elizabeth and Gina anyway. I can now amend the order with Govind for some additional ornamentation."

At a knock on the door, Luc automatically reached for his crutches. I couldn't blame him. My fingers wrapped around the hilt of my dagger, and knives sprang from sheaths hidden beneath Talbert's sleeves and into his hands.

Warden Tadhg opened the door, and Edberth entered with the tray of pastries he'd promised. Both he and the warden studiously ignored all of us, including Quan, sheathing our weapons.

"Thank you so much, Edberth," I said as I reached for one. I frowned as I noticed every single pastry had a bite torn out. I looked up at Luc's evening assistant.

His face heated. "I'm sorry, Chief Justice. All the wardens and the Ambassador's guards insisted on checking the food."

Luc rubbed his forehead while Talbert and Quan chuckled. I merely shook my head in weary resignation and bit into the almond pastry. "This tastes like Deborah's recipe," I said around the mouthful.

Edberth smiled gently. "Gifting me with a few of Deborah's recipes was the compromise High Brother Kam and Chief Justice Thalia came to when he tried to hire Deborah away from Balance."

I swallowed the suddenly hard lump of dough. "Please tell me you are jesting."

"I would never make light when it comes to a Temple's kitchen staff, m'lady." Edberth turned to Luc. "Do you need a fresh pot of tea, High Brother?"

"Yes, please, and an extra cup for Sister Shi Hua," Luc responded.

Edberth bowed and retreated from the room once again.

I held up the almond pastry. "I have half a mind to spit in Little Bear's porridge tomorrow morning."

"They're only trying to protect us," Luc said as he reached for a pastry before passing the platter to Talbert.

"No, they didn't have the manners to ask for some themselves," I muttered.

"I've warned my own wardens to be careful about any refreshment offered," Talbert said. He passed the platter to Quan, who held up his hand in polite refusal.

We were all quiet as we slowly consumed our treats and sipped our tea. The silence was preferable to acknowledging the uncomfortable truths we faced.

I was licking the last crumb from my thumb when there was another knock on the dining room door. This time, only the men grabbed their weapons. I grabbed another pastry.

Shi Hua entered followed by Edberth with a fresh pot of tea and an extra cup and plate.

Luc opened his mouth, but Shi Hua held up her right index finger.

"With all due respect, High Brother, don't say a word." Her finger made a sharp slashing motion. "Just don't."

"Chao?" I guessed.

She groaned and sat down next to me. "I swear my son knows as soon as I walk into my chambers. Mateqai had put him down to sleep a half candlemark before we returned."

A trill of part amusement, part resignation, and part sadness from Luc tickled my mind. The Issuran Temple of Light didn't allow women in their order, though many other nations did. It had been an adjustment for everyone in Orrin to have a priestess of Light, especially for Luc's staff. On the other hand, the priests and wardens quickly learned to take her seriously, especially when it came to unarmed combat in the practice yard.

Then the breeding edict came down from the home Temples last spring. Having a woman in the Temple had been bad enough. Having a baby like Chao caused more chaos than a demon incursion.

At least, the home Temple of Light hadn't insisted Luc try to sire another child after the loss of his and Sister Claudia of Love's unborn son. It had taken much counseling from Child for Luc and Claudia to deal with their grief. And even more counseling for me since my birth mother murdered the babe in an effort to fuel a demon spell to destroy the city of Orrin.

"Warden Mateqai missed his calling." I pulled the platter closer to Shi Hua.

She selected one of the pastries, stared at it, and examined the remaining treats. "Why do they all have bites missing?"

"Overprotective wardens," Talbert, Luc, and I said at the same time.

Edberth set the cup of tea he poured for Shi Hua in front of her. "I'll bring your eggs and cheese once you finished with your attempt to contact Jing." He bowed and left again.

"Are you all right, Sister?" Concern was an expression I'd never seen Quan wear, but he was obviously worried about Shi Hua.

She fixed him with a glare. "When you have children, and they poop and spit up on you and never let you sleep, then we will talk, Your Excellency."

Quan's left eyebrow rose, but she continued glaring at him. She was hardly a quiet, demure woman. However, she rarely snapped at anyone the way she had tonight.

Luc wouldn't correct her in front of members of other Temples. Talbert hid a slight smile behind his cup. And technically, I couldn't reprimand her since I was not her Temple seat. However, I could use one of High Sister Mya's techniques she used on me after a demon grimoire nearly drove me mad.

I laid my hand on her arm. "We're all scared of what might be happening in Chengzhou, none more than you and Po. However, lashing out at each other isn't going to help your friends and family."

She slumped in her chair. The pastry fell from her right hand, hit the edge of the table, and broke into multiple crumbs before hitting the hardwood floor.

I should have frozen time and rescued the treat. I couldn't bear the loss of an almond pastry.

"You're right, Lady Justice," Shi Hua murmured. "My apologies for my behavior, Your Excellency, High Brothers."

The Temple bells started tolling. Third Evening. Time to learn the truth.

If we could.

Chapter 5

When the final peal of the bells died, the five of us joined hands. Both Shi Hua and Quan's hands were clammy to the touch. In any other circumstance, I would have teased the ambassador about his nervousness, but I couldn't this time. Not with his family's lives at stake.

Luc and I gently fed energy into the young Jing priestess. Talbert and Quan focused on their desire to speak with Reverend Father Biming. Shi Hua launched her thread of magic westward.

The main problem was the Reverend Father was a quicksilver like Talbert. Someone who essentially was undetectable by those of us with mental talents. If the Reverend Father wasn't deliberately listening for Shi Hua, she wouldn't be able to communicate with him. Our unspoken hope was the demon attack meant he was listening for her.

Assuming the demons hadn't killed him.

Shi Hua? The masculine silent voice wasn't Biming. Nor was it Brother Jian of Light. From the feeling of two beings in one mind, he was a Wildling.

Fa? she asked. *Are you all right? Is Mei Wen alive? She said there was a demon attack in Chengzhou. Where's Reverend Father Biming?*

Just a moment, Fa said. The link still existed, but his attention was split. After a breathless moment, he returned. *I sent one of my wardens to fetch the Reverend Father. He assigned me to listen for you this morning.*

Brother Fa, Prince Po is with me, Shi Hua said. *As are Chief Justice Anthea and High Brothers Luc and Talbert.*

Your Highness, Honored Seats. I hope you don't mind, but Reverend Father Biming was adamant that he speak with you tonight. He will be here momentarily. The Jing priest hesitated a moment. *I can say a healer was already at the home Temple of Balance. The last report indicated Justice Mei Wen is alive.* His worry filtered through the link despite the young priest's best efforts. Shi Hua had told me she, Mei Wen, Jian, and Fa had been close when they were novices in the Jing capital.

How many justices did you lose, Brother Fa? I asked. *What assistance can Issura render?*

As to your first question, I do not know. Clergy and wardens are still searching Balance, m'lady. The young priest's weariness tugged on our link and I poured more of my own resources into Shi Hua. *As for your second, the Reverend Father can answer that question better than I can.*

The smooth essence of Reverend Father Biming entered our link. *Sister Shi Hua, are you all right? I was told you were in contact with Justice Mei Wen when the demons attacked Balance.*

I'm fine, Reverend Father, she reported. *Chief Justice Anthea absorbed the brunt of Justice Mei Wen's pain.*

Can we drop the titles for now, Biming? I said. *We have a multitude of questions, and I don't want to wear out Shi Hua more than necessary.*

I understand, Anthea, but may I please speak with Prince Po privately first? Biming said.

My brother and his sons are dead, aren't they? The tsunami of Quan's grief drowned all of us for a moment.

The empress as well, Your Highness. I am so sorry. Biming's love and affection for his prince swirled around our minds, muting a bit of Quan's despair.

How? I bit out.

One of the imperial concubines was replaced by a skinwalker. Biming's simple statement tore at me. When I first learned Shi Hua was Temple, she asked me how I was able to see demons. My strange sight that allowed me to see demons and skinwalkers resulted from an accident when I tried to bestow human sight on myself in my efforts to escape service to Balance. Shi Hua had hoped to replicate my spell, but according to my own Reverend Mother, all efforts to duplicate my accident had failed.

If I understood what I'd done wrong, I could have reproduced my eyesight in someone else. The emperor's little boys wouldn't be—

Anthea! Luc snapped. *You can wallow in guilt later.*

My apologies. I struggled to breathe evenly. From the anxiety irritating my nerves, I would need to visit High Sister Mya of Child before I would be able to sleep tonight. Both she and High Brother Ben of Vintner had been adamant that I couldn't rely on soma tears for sleep.

You must come home, Po, Biming said. *You are now the crown prince. The heads of the Temples know I'm speaking with you. We will keep the peace until you return.*

How bad is your situation? Talbert asked.

Biming gave a stark recitation of what he and the other Temple heads had pieced together over the last two candlemarks. The actual attacks matched Quan's analysis of quick, surgical strikes at the human institutions the demons considered their chief opposition. At the extent of the losses, I feared the almond pastries I'd eaten would make a reappearance.

Everyone of the Jing home Temples and their schools of philosophy had casualties. Of course, Light was more heavily targeted, but Balance and Death were as well. Which meant somehow the demons who survived the Battle of Tandor managed to get word to the other demons in our world before our own Crown Princess Chiara and the Issuran army hunted them down and killed them.

The School of the Dragon and the Phoenix suffered the most casualties. According to Quan, they were an offshoot based on the more esoteric teachings of Balance and Light. His own father had been a master of the school and its representative in the imperial court until he was struck with a scourge designed to resemble the disease known as the Child's Curse.

The teams of clergy and talents who acted as the imperial family's personal bodyguards had been killed by the skinwalker, as had a number of the imperial harem. The skinwalker killed as many of the civilian troops guarding the imperial palace as it could before a cook warded it in one of the kitchens until Temple assistance arrived and ended the threat.

All the guilds were ignored by the demons except for the Healers Guild. One master, a journeyman, and a handful of apprentices survived at their headquarters, but in the demons' focus on the main guild house, they missed the personnel who'd taken up residency at the Temples to assist with the multitude of babes the breeding edict had produced.

I wondered if the demons targeted the Healers Guild because it spawned off from the Temple of Death. Balance was the only one of the Twelve Temples that didn't have a guild cleave off from the order over the last century.

The demons also ignored the nobles. If Jing were like Issura, few of the nobles had any active talents. Our enemies needed to take out the Temples, the guilds, and the schools of philosophy. Everyone else could be eaten at their leisure.

Quan let out an audible sigh before he said silently, *It's the midwinter, and Issura has been beset with storms since the solstice.*

We may not be able to get you a weather sorcerer, but we can petition the duke for a weather oracle, Talbert said.

If Anthea and I ask, the duke may be willing to loan us Captain Titus and the Mars Tranquilus, Luc added. *She's a nimble ship with an excellent crew, and no offense, Quan, but she can handle a winter storm better than your ship can.*

Quan chuckled, but the effort sounded forced. *You have no argument from me on that score.*

In the morning and with your permission, Quan, I said. *Shi Hua and I can contact Queen Teodora, report Jing's situation, and petition for additional aid.*

If it's all right with you, Anthea, I'd like to be involved in that conversation, Quan replied.

The renegades' spies are expecting you to go back to Jing, Talbert said. *There's going to be ambushes along the way.*

In the middle of the Peaceful Sea? I said.

Yes, my dear Anthea, Quan mocked. *They are called pirates.*

We have to assume they will strike before you leave Issura, Luc said. *I strongly suggest you stay here at the Temple of Light for your own safety.*

I concur, sir, Shi Hua said.

What about my father? Quan asked.

I'll speak with High Sister Mya, Talbert said. *Assuming you have no objection about moving him to the Temple of Child, Your Highness?*

Thank you, Quan said.

Can we get the crown prince out of Orrin within the next day? Shi Hua asked.

It will be at least a day and a half, assuming the duke agrees with our request. Luc was right. With the preparations Captain Titus would need to make for the two-month voyage across the Peaceful Sea, he couldn't launch his ship before the late morning high tide on First Day. So much for the quiet of Rest Day.

No comment, Anthea? Quan teased.

Only if you say no to common sense precautions, I replied. *You already know those from Thief will not be as direct even though they agree with me.* Biming's laughter pealed like a bell through my mind. It sounded like he needed the emotional release.

We'll discuss our preparations further tomorrow at the same time,

Biming said. *I'll send Jian and Fa with a Temple group I trust to meet you in Ryukyu. Is that acceptable, Shi Hua?*

The sister had come to Issura as Quan's bodyguard. It said much that Biming trusted her to get their new emperor back to Chengzhou safely.

Yes, sir, she replied without hesitation. It hadn't registered yet that her new assignment meant leaving her son Chao behind, possibly never seeing him again. *In all my jealousy over the other Light and Balance clergy given permission to bear children, the thought of leaving my child behind hadn't occurred to me.*

Mya never called me self-centered during our talks involving my emotional repair work. She should have. Maybe I would have understood sooner.

Be careful, Biming, I said. *Renegades may still be hiding in and around Chengzhou.*

We will, Anthea. Weariness filled his mental voice even though it was fairly early in the day for Jing, but a demon attack can exhaust everyone when the initial adrenaline charge fades.

Shi Hua dissolved the link with Biming and Fa. She blinked a few times to reorient herself. "Shall I inform your concubine to have her order the embassy household to pack, Your Highness?"

Quan nodded absently as he played with the beads on his moustache. "Wait." He gestured sharply. "Hers and her son's belongings. Sufficient clothes and weapons to sustain me during the voyage. Have Mistress Yin Li select four guards to accompany us. No more, no less. Tell her about—" He choked on the word while he did his best to be the world leader he thought he should be. "—about the imperial family, but neither of you are to say anything to anyone else. Understood?"

"Yes, Your Highness." She nodded.

"It's going to be difficult to keep this news quiet, Po," I said softly. "Not with the clergy from all Twelve Temples present tonight when the demons attacked Chengzhou."

"I trust the seats of Orrin to keep their silence and to ask those of their Temples to do the same." He flashed me a brief smile. "At least until I can leave Orrin."

"I'll ride up to the duke's estate." Luc grabbed his crutches and stood.

"Tonight? I thought I was the one with the lack of manners," I teased.

"Luc's right." Talbert pushed to his feet as well. "We need to work fast to get the new emperor out of Issura alive. I'll inform the other seats of what's happening."

"What about me?" I was a little nonplussed the two high brothers had taken the jobs I would have preferred.

"You and I will put together a list of requirements I may need from your Teodora," Quan answered. "We both need to be prepared for to-morrow morning. Would you mind if the chief justice and I use your dining room for a little while longer, High Brother?"

Luc nodded. "Our facilities are at your disposal, Your Highness. And I'll have Edberth brew you two some more tea."

Quan was correct. We did need to be prepared for speaking with the queen. But what puzzled me was the surprising lack of jealousy from Luc for once over me spending time alone with the future emperor of Jing.

Maybe Luc was simply happy Quan would soon be out of his hair.

In my case, I simply didn't like change, and I'd had far too much of it over the last two winters.

And some instinct deep in my spirit said Balance wasn't done fling-ing more challenges at me than She already had.

Chapter 6

Apparently, Talbert had stopped at Balance to let the other three justices know we had confirmed the demon attack in Jing and that Mei Wen still lived. However, he also told them I would return shortly to fill them in on the specifics.

All three women were wide awake and sitting in our receiving room when I returned to our Temple shortly after First Night. Sivan served us a nice bottle of Pana red before I settled down with the other justices and our chief wardens to relay what I had learned.

Gina whistled when I finished my recitation. "This is, this is . . ." She shook her head as words failed her.

"It was only a matter of time before they tried something bigger than taking over Tandor—" Erato started.

"I beg your pardon." By Elizabeth's tone, she was definitely offended. I couldn't blame her. Especially not after all the horrors the skinwalkers and the renegades had inflicted on her for a year before we discovered what had happened in her former city.

"Their silent, careful plan failed," Erato growled. "So a strategy of this magnitude was needed. I would say the same thing if they had attacked Standora. Take out the queen and her daughters and spouses—" The justice's fist clenched on the tabletop, and the bitter essence of her fury banged against my mental shields.

"We have no indication the queen and her family are in danger," Yanaba said gently.

"But there's been a concerted effort to assassinate distance speakers associated with our nations' leaders for the last several months," I stated. "Cut off lines of communication and launch these attacks at specific targets." I leaned my elbows on the surface of the table as I worked through their logic. "The renegades had to have developed this scheme. Demons don't think like this."

"And you know how demons think?" Erato's words were sharper than a freshly honed knife edge.

"Yes," the rest of the people in the room answered.

I didn't want to get into the subject of how I knew. "Their normal tactic is to overwhelm an opponent with sheer numbers. They've relied on that for nine centuries, and we've managed to fight them back every time."

"Because of Balance's warning and the Temples' unity," Yanaba said.

"And the renegades have been trying to break that unity between recruitment and assassination of the clergy," Little Bear growled.

"Throw in a little torture while you're at it, Chief Warden," Elizabeth said dryly.

"Yanaba, I need you to—" I began.

"To cover the court cases for you on First Day." Humor laced her voice. "It's winter, Anthea. You don't need to feel guilty. You're not dumping your work on me, and Xander would love to spend time with Kosumi."

"You only have a declaration of last wishes on the docket." Elizabeth laughed.

"I'd rather that than dealing with Ambassador, I mean, Crown Prince Po," Yanaba retorted.

I groaned. "Did he proposition you?"

"No," she said. "But he just lost most of his family. All the crown prince has left is his father, and from what Shi Hua told me, his father's health has steadily declined over the last year. He won't survive the trip home to Jing even if the crown prince was so inclined to take his father home with him."

"Getting the ambassador home is going to be extremely difficult to do." Little Bear tapped the fingers of his right hand on the tabletop. "The Jing nobility were adamant Quan not be named as the empress's successor."

"Mainly because his latent talent was a Thief ability." I lifted my cup. "Then there was the rivalry between the imperial consort and the senior Quan's respective schools of philosophy." I took a sip. Even at this late hour, the wine didn't take the edge off my nerves.

"Which means there's going to be assassins after the crown prince—" Little Bear's face reddened at my not-so-subtle correction of Quan's new title. "—in order for the different factions to seize the throne. The Temples in Jing aren't going to be able to stay neutral. At least, not for long."

"Perhaps a compromise could be reached," Erato said. "Jing allows women into their Light order. What if he married a priestess willing to leave the Temples?"

An argument erupted among the justices and wardens about what it would take for the Jing Reverend Father of Light to agree to such a madcap plan.

A shiver ran through me. It explained why Quan wanted to talk to Crown Princess Chiara and her husband White Eagle, the current duke of Standora, tomorrow. The duke had been a priest in Conflict and been given disposition to leave Conflict and marry Chiara. The new emperor of Jing was already planning his next steps.

That was assuming we could keep him alive long enough to take the throne.

The next day at Second Morning, I brought Erato with me to Light even though it was Rest Day. She was smart though her personality could be a bit prickly at times. The difference between her and me at the same age was the unhealthy amount of resentment I'd carried. I'd always blamed Balance for taking me from my mother, but reading between the lines of the Balance records, my grandmother Chief Justice Thalia had been desperate to get me away from Gerd before she tried to harm me again.

I wondered how Thalia would have reacted if she knew I took Gerd's head for practicing demon magic.

The rain had stopped over night, but a chill wind swept inland from the Peaceful Sea. Not cold enough to freeze the remaining water on the ground, but with the moisture still in the air, it was the uncomfortable cold that settled deep in one's bones even with the short walk from Balance to Light.

When we entered the Temple's sanctuary, braziers glowed white hot. They matched the blinding light from the oil fed eternal flame in front of the blue statue of Light Himself. The Light head of household Istaqa waited to greet us, no doubt warned by both the Temple's royal guest and the warden standing guard at the Temple steps.

Istaqa bowed. "The high brother and Crown Prince Po are waiting for you in the high brother's dining room, Chief Justice."

Damn. The word was out about Quan's true identity, at least among the Temple personnel. However, there were no worshippers currently in the sanctuary, and Istaqa was a stickler for protocol.

I inclined my head in return. "Thank you, Istaqa." I glanced at Wardens Ahiga and Daniel who had accompanied us across the boulevard. None of the clergy could go anywhere outside of their own Temples without a warden escort due to the rash of assassination attempts last year.

Balance help me, I couldn't even use a privy without being accompanied by a warden on the nights the clergy gathered for entertainment during the winter.

While our wardens remained in the sanctuary, Istaqa led us to the dining room before he took our cloaks. Quan and Shi Hua were already there. Surprisingly, so was Luc.

"I asked the high brother to join this conversation," Quan said softly.

I looked at Luc again.

He shrugged and smiled. "I knew I couldn't keep the sister forever."

I sighed and led Erato to a chair. Once she was settled in her seat, I dropped into the one between her and Luc. He poured tea from the pot in front of him. Yellow steam drifted from the cup he handed me. It quickly turned green and dissipated. I took Erato's hand in mine and wrapped her fingers around the warm orange-yellow ceramic cup.

"Still no word on additional personnel for you?" I asked as I accepted my own cup from Luc.

"Not yet." Silently, he added, *We'll discuss this later.*

He was correct. This wasn't a matter to be debated in front of non-Temple people, much less a foreign dignitary.

"All right, but since I was dragged out into the cold—" I eyed Shi Hua. "—I want some play time with little Chao before I leave."

She chuckled. "I expected such a request. He should be awake be the time we finish here, Chief Justice."

"As long as you don't expect him to interact with you," Quan teased. "Yin Shang was terribly disappointed Chao cannot play with toys yet."

I rubbed my arms from the shiver that ran through me. Just like me, Chao was born in Issura with Temple-level talent. He might never be able to visit his mother's homeland.

"Should I ask Istaqa for another brazier?" Luc frowned at me.

"No, I'm fine." I smiled at him. "I'm tired. It was a long night."

"You're more gracious than Lady Katarina." He grinned.

I tensed. "What did the duke say about borrowing the *Mars Tranquilus*?"

"The good high brother used his role as the future duke's godfather to bargain down the price for using the ship." Quan laughed.

"And?" I prompted at Luc's odd expression.

"Duke Marco's condition for using the *Mars Tranquilus* is that one of us must accompany the prince to Jing," Luc said sourly.

"He what?" I stared at Luc.

Erato burst out laughing. Shi Hua tittered into her cup. Quan simply grinned.

Luc shrugged again. "It's better than his lady wife's suggested recompense."

I leaned back in my chair. "I don't want to know. Should we get this over with?"

"Eager to get rid of me so soon, Chief Justice?" Quan wore his lascivious leer. I had not seen that particular expression in almost a year. No doubt he hoped to get one last rise out of me. Sad to say, I would miss our diplomatic and personal sparring.

Not that I'd ever admit such to him.

"I anticipate the next Jing ambassador to Issura will be far more charming," I said. "Who knows? If the breeding edict is still in effect, I may try to forge deeper bonds with your nation."

Quan slapped his hand against his chest. "Alas, you wound me, m'lady!"

I'm not happy either, Luc said. His irritation prickled along his silent speech, though no one at the table would notice his true feelings from his expression.

We'll discuss this later, I replied.

Shi Hua and I reached for the hands of the people on each side of us. Once the five of us joined, the Jing priestess sent a pulse of magic in the direction of Standora.

Greetings, Sister Shi Hua. Our queen, the crown princess, and the duke of Standora are with me.

Odd. The queen rarely participated in these conversations. I'd understand if she already knew about Emperor Chengwu and his son's assassinations. In such a case, she would speak directly with another nation's ruler. I tried to tamper my suspicions the royals had been informed already about last night's events.

Good morntide, Lord Ayatulutul. Shi Hua recited who participated in the link on our end, but she hesitated when she came to Quan. *And Crown Prince Po of Jing*, she finally said.

What has happened? Duke White Eagle demanded.

I ran through the events of the previous evening, including our conversation with Reverend Father Biming.

We share your grief, Prince Po, Queen Teodora said. The wave of empathy from those in Standora added weight to the traditional words. *What aid may we render other than getting you home as soon as possible?*

Duke Marco of Orrin has graciously offered the service of his fastest ship and his best crew, Quan answered. *However, I have a personal request. I would like Chief Justice Anthea and High Brother Luc to escort me back to Jing.*

My jaw dropped. Luc's own shock echoed through my mind and rippled down my spine.

May I ask why? Queen Teodora's curiosity swept through the link.

Now, why wasn't the queen surprised? But it wasn't a question I could ask through the link. The queen didn't tolerate impertinence, and I rather liked keeping my own head attached to my neck.

Because I have before and still trust them with my life, Quan stated. *I have no doubt the attack on Chengzhou was meant to disrupt Jing and our alliances with other nations such as your own queendom. There's no question in my mind traps will be laid on our journey west. Furthermore, I agree with the Matriarch of Diné. They are your best diplomatic representatives in that I know whatever they say, it will not run counter to your own intentions. Finally, I was in Tandor during the demon siege. I know they will do whatever they must to get me home to Chengzhou.*

So you wish them to represent Issura at your coronation? There was a teasing quality in the queen's mental tone.

If that is acceptable with you, Your Majesty, he replied far more soberly. *I do have some questions for you beyond protocol, and I wish for your advice since my own blessed mother is no longer with us.*

I am honored by your request, the queen responded.

I withdrew from the link at the same time as Erato. From the way Luc was blinking, he'd withdrawn, too. But when I looked at Shi Hua, she wore a frown.

"He didn't keep you in the link?" I asked.

"No." Her short answer indicated how displeased she was. Shi Hua had been Quan's personal body guard for six years before I begged for her to be temporarily transferred to the Orrin Temple of Light. We'd lost so many clergy and wardens in the last year, and frankly, Luc needed the help because he sure as Balance wasn't getting it from his own Reverend Father Farrell.

"The circumstances have changed for all of us, Sister," I said softly. "He still values your contributions."

Shi Hua stared at the tabletop. "I fear I won't be able to keep him alive long enough to ascend to the throne."

"We won't let that happen." Erato attempted to instill confidence in the young Jing priestess, but it was an empty promise, and we all knew it.

Shi Hua forced a smile. "I doubt if Queen Teodora will allow me to keep all of you in Jing until the new emperor dies peacefully in his old age." She sobered. "The queen wishes you three to rejoin the link."

I closed my eyes and let Shi Hua pull me into the conversation.

Is there anything else you wish to discuss with me, Prince Po? Queen Teodora said.

No, Your Majesty, Quan replied. *Again, I appreciate your wise counsel.*

Then, may I speak privately to my own subjects for a moment, Your Highness? she said.

Of course, Quan replied. He and Shi Hua withdrew from the link, so Lord Ayatulutul had to carry the bulk of the work once again.

Chief Justice, High Brother, do you two trust Justice Erato? Duke White Eagle asked.

Her fingers tensed in my grip. I couldn't blame her, and I was sure I'd hear about this later.

Yes, I replied. *However, if she makes a misstep while I'm in Jing, I trust Justice Yanaba more to deal with her appropriately.*

I felt rather than heard Erato's gasp of dismay. Apparently, she assumed I had been embellishing when I told her of some of the problems among the Temples. To be faced with the distrust of the royal family had to be a major blow to her ego.

Justice Erato does need seat experience if we are to continue our fight with the renegades and the demons which is why I included her in today's meeting, I added.

Very well, the queen said. *What's the real reason Crown Prince Po wants you two to accompany him to Jing? And that's assuming I let you two go with him.*

Honestly, Your Majesty, we've saved his arse more than once. While Luc's tone was respectful, he was obviously done mincing words. *He believes that between his two personal bodyguards, Chief Justice Anthea, and me, we can keep him alive long enough to take the throne.*

How bad are things in Jing right now? Crown Princess Chiara asked.

They've had more than their share of trouble with the renegades thanks to a couple of their philosophy schools, Luc said. *Add in the nobility being unhappy the prince's minor talent in Thief. That's the reason his mother named his younger brother as heir. The fact that Reverend Father Biming is shaken by the speed and ferocity of the strikes at the palace and the Temples tells us things are more dire than his words indicate.*

I'm more concerned with High Brother Luc and Sister Shi Hua leaving, Duke White Eagle said. *Orrin's Temple of Light is already understaffed, and they are now in the position of guarding our southern border.*

What if we don't go through Reverend Father Farrell? I said. *There's a couple of priestesses who would have been assigned to Light if we followed the same protocols as other nations.*

Like Jing? the duke teased.

We are crippling our chances to stop the demons for once and all with our short-sightedness, Your Grace, Luc said.

I whole-heartedly agree, but I also don't want to make enemies with other Temples, White Eagle said.

I would suggest Sister Claudia of Love, I said. *She is High Sister Dragonfly's second, but I don't believe either the high sister or the Reverend Mother of Love would object to a temporary assignment to Light.*

Luc's surprise tickled my mind. I'd definitely be hearing about this later. But despite my misplaced jealousy of Claudia, she was a good person and would do whatever it took to support Luc's own second Jeremy. Not to mention, it would be good to have a feminine touch to assist him with his son since Shi Hua had to return to Jing.

Who else? Crown Princess Chiara asked.

I would want High Mother Leocadia if we didn't finally have a stable seat at her Temple, Luc said. *But there's another priestess she brought with her to Orrin with Light abilities, Mother Kalama. High Mother Leocadia would agree, but I cannot vouch for her Reverend Mother.*

What about Balance? the crown princess asked. *Our understanding is Chief Justice Elizabeth will be headed to the Duchy of Anacapa shortly after the Spring Rituals. I don't like the idea of Yanaba alone.*

With the early snows, Justice Erato and Brother Wolf Run were forced to winter in the city, I said. *They will be here until the road to Mountain Gate is passable, which if the duke's weather oracle is correct, won't be until two weeks after the Spring Rituals.*

That's going to put a dent in our trade with the Plains Nations for a second year in a row, White Eagle said.

The weather is currently beyond our control, my love, Crown Princess Chiara teased.

In the meantime, Chief Justice Elizabeth and I will do everything we can to assist Justice Yanaba and Brother Jeremy of Light while the chief justice and the high brother escort Prince Po home, Erato assured the royals.

But, Your Majesty, we can't just leave our posts without notice to the home Temples, I protested. Now why in Balance was I suddenly concerned about propriety? Before I became the seat of Orrin, I would have jumped at the chance to irritate Reverend Mother Alara.

We don't tell the Reverend Mothers and Fathers until you have left Issura. Queen Teodora sounded quite decisive on that matter. *You will send notice to your home Temples by courier since Prince Po has asked for the return of his distance speaker, and I have a standing order for your diplomatic presence in Jing based on a recommendation from the Matriarch of Diné. Unfortunately, I lost my own distance speaker recently and have not replaced her so you could not give me immediate notice to relay to them, and the crown prince needed to leave immediately.*

This was one of the reasons I hated politics, but given Reverend Mother Alara's odd behavior and Reverend Farrell's obsession with Love priestesses and his jealousy of Luc, I didn't blame the queen. She probably saw more of their erratic behavior than she cared to. From the edge in her voice, she was still angry about the assassination of her previous distance speaker last autumn. Nor had she made it public knowledge she had a replacement.

With all due respect, Your Majesty, I would hate to destroy our relationship with Love by not informing Reverend Mother Sxa'min right away, I said. *She's been rather helpful in delivering information through High Sister Dragonfly.*

I can smooth the feathers on this end, White Eagle said. *Just make sure you include Prince Po's request for your presence in a message to the queen.*

Yes, Your Grace, I said. *Is there anything else we need to do to assist you, Your Majesty?*

Yes, there is, Chief Justice, Queen Teodora answered. *I need you and High Brother Luc to come home alive.*

Chapter 7

I blinked as the link dissolved, a little surprised to find Quan and Shi Hua still sitting at the table in Luc's private dining room. The slight vertigo from lengthy distance speaking made me nauseated.

"Are you all right, Anthea?" Luc peered at me, and his concern lapped at my mental shields.

"Yes." I held up a hand. "I've been doing too much distance speaking lately."

Erato fidgeted next to me. She obviously had plenty of questions, but she was keeping her silence for now.

"Well?" Quan prompted. "What did Queen Teodora say? Is she agreeable to you two accompanying us back to Jing?"

"Yes," Luc said. "However, the chief justice and I have much to accomplish in a very short time despite it being Rest Day. As do you, Your Highness."

Quan rose. "Thank you, High Brother. I am deeply indebted to you and the chief justice as well as Duke Marco." He left the dining room.

"Shi Hua?" Luc said quietly.

She straightened in her chair. "What do you require, High Brother?"

"Go spend time with Chao while you can," he said gently.

She nodded, leapt from her chair, and raced out of the dining room. Her emotional turmoil battered the magic inherent in the stones of the Temple. It sent a peel of distress through me like the whistles only dogs could hear.

"I won't steal any of her time with the baby," I murmured.

"She may not appreciate your sentiment in her current state," Luc said. "But I do."

"I knew she couldn't stay in Orrin forever." My eyes burned. "I should never have put her in this position."

"It wasn't your fault, Chief Justice," Erato squeezed my fingers. "She would have still been in the city when the edict came down from the home Temples. She would have been ordered to fulfill it even if she were still acting as the prince's bodyguard."

"What about you and Brother Wolf Run?" I asked.

She released my hand and laughed. "He's been sowing his seed in every village in our circuit since the edict came down."

"Well, he is an attractive young man," Luc said.

I frowned at him. "Are you planning to switch your bed partner preferences?"

"I'm simply happy Child has given me an exemption," he growled.

Death, take me now. Once again, I'd taken the wrong step in my teasing. Every time I believed things were back to normal between us, reality slapped me. "My apologies. I misspoke, High Brother."

"No, you didn't." He held up his hands. "I'm the one who should apologize. I'm taking my anger over my own situation out on you." He inclined his head. "I'm sorry, Chief Justice."

When I remained silent, he examined my fellow justice. "Is there anything we can do to help you before we leave, Erato? You and Brother Wolf Run will be departing for your circuit before Anthea and I return."

She sighed and carefully set her cup on the scarred tabletop. "I don't wish to seem ungrateful, High Brother, but may I ask Brother Jeremy for his company after Sister Shi Hua leaves? I've lain with Brother Hawk at Chumash Way every time we passed through, but I haven't had any luck."

Chumash Way was the last town on the Issuran side of the Kul-shra'jek Pass. Heaven's Gate was the last town on the Comanche side. The pass itself was considered neutral territory. If anyone tried to live in the pass, they would need plenty of supplies because it became impassible from the Autumn Equinox until shortly before the Spring Rituals in most years. The only reason Light kept a small Temple in Chumash Way was to process the incoming traders and collect merchant taxes.

"You've lain with him more than one time a visit?" I asked.

Her index finger tapped the side of her cup. "Yes, m'lady. We've even been timing our visits with my fertility cycles as well as staying an extra day or two, but no luck. It's part of the reason I originally wanted to stay in Orrin a couple of extra days. I consulted with the Healers Guild, but Chief Healer Aaron said there is no reason I cannot conceive."

I made a dismissive noise in the back of my throat. "Did you also speak with Master Bly?" I trusted Aaron with my life, but he had a tendency to not think outside of the Guild teachings. Bly had a talent for looking at a problem from all angles.

Erato smiled. "Actually, the chief healer called her in for my examination. He was concerned he may have missed something given my number of attempts. Master Bly made the suggestion the issue may be with Brother Hawk's seed, and not with my fertility."

"I'm assuming none of the other priestess's have been able to conceive with him," I asked.

"Not that I'm aware of." Erato chuckled softly. "But then they were more interested in attracting Wolf Run's attention."

"Too much familiarity with Brother Hawk?" I asked.

Luc laughed. "More like Hawk isn't as young and pretty as Wolf Run."

When I looked at him askance, he admitted, "I believe Hawk is over seventy winters."

"This is his seventy-first," Erato said. "And I don't understand why other women would put such a premium on appearances. Hawk is very sweet and kind and gentle as a lover."

"You're totally correct, my dear Erato," Luc said with no humor. "Those of us with sight make judgments in regards to appearances, while those of Balance put more weight on actions and words."

"I don't think we should be the ones to give Erato advice on such things," I said. "Not to mention there are dispatches I need to stamp out before morning." I pushed to my feet. "Do you wish to stay, Erato?"

"No, thank you, m'lady." She stood as well. "I don't wish to intrude on Jeremy and Shi Hua's short time left."

"Thank you for your hospitality, High Brother." I nodded to Luc before I reached for my fellow justice's hand once again to guide her from the private dining room. "How soon will we have a departure time?"

"I should know any moment," he said. "I shall send a squire to inform you once the duke sends me a messenger."

"Thank you," I murmured.

Erato and I left the room and walked to the sanctuary. Once we donned our winter cloaks and exited the Temple of Light, she leaned close and whispered, "May I ask you a private question, m'lady?"

"If you don't mind that I ask you one in return."

Erato switched to silent speech. *Was I wrong to choose Brother Hawk? It had not occurred to me his seed would not work. There was a case I adjudicated where the seed father was in his nineties and the woman he impregnated was younger than me.*

No, you weren't wrong, I answered. *Those chosen by Balance were never taught how to pick a suitable seed father because we weren't supposed to bear children.*

I hesitated a moment before I added, *May I ask why you and Wolf Run haven't tried?*

She giggled. *He's not just my spiritual partner. We have the same birth parents.*

Oh. My apologies. This seems to be my day for verbal missteps.

Erato laughed in earnest. *It's not a subject my brother and I adver- tise, but I have the impression our Reverend Mother didn't want the same situation our predecessors on the Eastern Orrin circuit found themselves.*

Did you know she manipulated me? I complained.

No, but I'm not surprised. Erato remained silent until we reached the top steps of the Temple of Balance. *Have you heard anything about Justice Melanippe?*

I had to rein in my natural suspicion. *Nothing from the home Temple. The last time I saw her was our own ordination. May I inquire why?*

She was my mentor when I was a novice.

We entered the Temple and shed our winter cloaks before Erato continued.

Melanippe and I continued exchanging letters when I was assigned to the Eastern Orrin circuit. Erato's worry nibbled on my psyche. *The last letter I received from her was dated shortly after midsummer.*

"Nathan?" I said.

"Yes, Lady Justice," he said from beneath the pile of damp winter wear.

"After you've hung up our cloaks, would you please tell Sivan to bring Justice Erato and me a pot of tea to my office?"

"Yes, Lady Justice." My squire scampered in the direction of the cloak room, and I noticed there was a definite gap between his leggings and his indoor footwear.

"Yes, Sivan knows," Little Bear whispered from my left. "She's been trading clothing with Death's head of household in order to keep the squires properly attired."

I shook my head. "We're going to have similar issues with Kosumi, and he's going to grow just as fast as Nathan and Ming Wei."

"If not faster." My chief warden chuckled. "May I request a bit of your time after you're done with Justice Erato?"

"No." I already knew the speech he was about to deliver. It was the same one he'd given me before I left for Diné last fall.

"With all due respect—" he began.

"I don't have the time to waste, Chief Warden," I snapped.

"I merely wanted to review procedures with you and Justice Yanaba prior to your departure," he said. "And Sivan already threatened my manhood if I gave you a difficult time over not taking me on this voyage."

I relented. "In that case, yes, I can meet with you and Justice Yanaba."

Before Little Bear could add more to my plate, I wrapped Erato's left fingers about my elbow once again and led her to my office. I had her settled and taken my own chair when Sivan strode into my office with a tray.

I relaxed at the sweet smell of Jing black tea. Maybe I could wrestle an additional tea concession from Quan for escorting him home.

Once Sivan poured our beverages and left, I considered how to word things with Erato. We'd already gone through truthspelling her and Wolf Run when they arrived in Orrin for restocking after the Spring Rituals and at midsummer. But then, we were all paranoid after what had happened to Tandor, and we truthspelled them yet again when they had to turn back after the early winter snows in the Gray Mountains.

"Was there anything odd or suspicious in Melanippe's letters over the past year?" I sipped my cup.

Erato's skin shifted from bright yellow to a greenish cast. "She would never join the renegades!"

"I'm not saying she did," I said. "No one has seen her for months."

Erato tilted her head. "I do not understand, Anthea. Those who instruct at the home Temple rarely leave. With the recent demon incursions—" A half-cry, half-sob erupted from her as her logic shouted the truth she'd suppressed in her fear. The cup slipped from her hands, bounced off the edge of my desk, and shattered against the marble floor.

Chapter 8

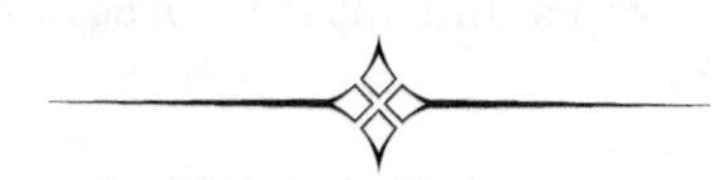

My office door burst open. Warden Gina practically jumped into the room with her dagger in her hand.

"At ease!" I barked before she did anything stupid. "Justice Erato's cup slipped from her grasp. Please have Nathan fetch some rags and broom so we can clean up this mess."

Gina exhaled and sheathed her dagger. "My apologies, Justices. You scared the demon out of me."

I made a shooing motion, and Gina departed, calling for Nathan as she went.

"Did I ruin any documents?" Erato sniffed as she struggled to control her emotions.

"No." I rose and rounded my desk. Orange liquid stained the blue cloth covering her legs and spread in a widening pool beneath the soles of her boots. "Your robes and the floor took the brunt of the tea. Don't move."

I checked her hands and legs for any cuts or burns. "Are you all right?"

"Not exactly." She sniffed again. "I'm so sorry. I'm usually more careful."

"There's nothing to apologize for," I said softly.

"Balance help me, are you both all right?" Sivan rushed into my office with a clean mug. Nathan followed on her heels with a bucket and rags.

"We're fine," I said as I moved out of my squire's way. "Nathan, take care. The glaze on those mugs can be sharper than a knife."

I bit my tongue when Sivan repeated my evaluation of Erato's well-being. Maybe my visits with Mya were helping me keep my temper in check after all.

"Give me your robes, Justice," Sivan demanded. "I'll fetch a clean set from your quarters."

Before Erato could answer, Sivan had untied the laces and removed the garment. Erato wrapped her arms about her torso at the sudden chill since she only wore a silk tunic. Sivan strode from my office with the damp robes.

Nathan straightened. "Do you need anything else, Chief Justice?"

"No, thank you," I said. He left with the bucket of broken pieces and tea-soaked rags while I retrieved a spare blanket I kept in a weapons trunk in my office. The woolen wrap was a safer way to keep warm instead of bringing a brazier into my office with all the parchment and papyrus in the room.

"Here." I unfolded the blanket and wrapped it around Erato's shoulders. "This will keep you warm until Sivan comes back."

I'm sorry for not keeping my composure, Chief Justice, she said silently.

Actually, you've given me an excuse to raise some inquiries, I replied. *If you don't mind. That way you and Yanaba can do some quiet checking with the other justices you personally know.*

I don't understand why someone at the home Temple didn't tell me about her disappearance with all the letters I've been sending, she said.

I poured tea into the new cup and placed it carefully in her hands. *The Reverend Mother is restricting information as she tries to ferret out the spy within her walls. We believe Melanippe may have discovered who the renegade is and was killed.*

It wasn't the exact truth, but it was close enough. Erato didn't need to know I found out about Melanippe's disappearance through Thief.

Balance help me, I received more information from the crown and the other Temples than I did from my own superior. Was Reverend Mother Alara attempting to keep rigid control of her people, or was something else going on at the home Temple?

What can I do to help? Erato asked.

Keep sending letters to Melanippe, I said as I resumed my seat in my own chair. *Say whatever you would have if I hadn't told you what happened.*

That seems to be a huge waste of parchment, but I will, Erato said.

I know, but it may be a way to flush out our spy. However, please be careful. We've already lost one justice. I don't want to lose you as well. I wished I felt as sure about this plan as I projected to Erato.

But I feared the attack on Chengzhou was only a harbinger of what was about to come.

Chapter 9

I had just completed the dispatches I needed to send to the capital when Magistrate DiCook arrived. Normally, we had our weekly meeting on First Day, but I had no doubt Duke Marco had informed him of the upcoming departure of the *Mars Tranquilus*. There had been a time when DiCook and I were constantly at loggerheads. It was amazing how murder and demons could change one's relationships.

It also helped our Temple's cook Deborah was more proficient in the kitchen than his own wife. He contrived reasons to meet at Balance around meal times so often that I suggested a permanent weekly appointment. Yet another reason he would lose his temper about me being gone for several months. I would have to suggest he have the same meeting on First Day with Yanaba.

Sivan brought the midday meal to my office. Thankfully, she said nothing about last night or this morning's orders, but before I could address the upcoming changes, DiCook said, "So why is the *Mars Tranquilus* really preparing to set sail? The duke wouldn't tell me."

Damn, I was going to miss his bluntness while I traveled to Jing.

"And you're not one to relinquish a chance to come to Balance for a meal," I replied.

"Happy coincidence." He picked up his spoon. "But my job is to keep track of unusual happenings in Orrin. Sailors and shoremen loading provisions on Rest Day is definitely unusual."

I leaned my elbows on the small table I kept in my office for these sorts of meetings. "There was a demon attack in Chengzhou last night."

"I figured that one out on my own, but why would Ambassador Quan be recalled over . . ." DiCook's voice trailed off as he put the pieces together. He set his spoon back in his bowl of venison stew before he started cursing. "Who all knows?"

"Duke Marco, Captain Titus, and every member of the clergy who attended the Mill tournament at Thief last night," I replied.

"I beg your pardon?" DiCook looked both alarmed and confused. "You haven't informed the queen or your own Reverend Mother?"

"I finished stamping out the letters to them both before you arrived." I hated withholding information from him, so I distracted myself by pouring him a cup of wine. After last night, my stomach couldn't handle any heavy drink. Thankfully, Sivan had brought a fresh pot of peppermint tea to soothe my recalcitrant digestive system. "What's your opinion of Justice Yanaba?"

"She's come a long way over the last year . . ." Once again, his voice trailed off as his cognitive abilities caught up with his words. Another set of curses fell from his lips. "Reverend Mother Alara is reassigning you since the poor child can't leave the city walls."

Yanaba's strange situation had been a problem for nearly a year. In her attempt to destroy the demons that attacked the Temple of Balance last spring, she had overextended her abilities to the point her psyche left her body and merged with the city itself. Shi Hua, Jeremy, and Brother Turtle from Child managed to untangle Yanaba's spirit from her spell. But the cost was Yanaba's inability to take more than a step or two through Orrin's gates.

Normally, a junior justice is assigned to a senior position after their two years of apprenticing with a chief justice. But poor Yanaba may have to spend the rest of her life here in the city of Orrin.

"I am leaving Issura," I said dryly. "But not by the Reverend Mother's orders. What I'm about to tell you cannot leave my office, Malven."

The fact that I used DiCook's given name shook some sense into him. "Quan wants you to accompany him back to Jing."

"He seems to believe I can keep him alive long enough for him to take the imperial throne." I sipped my tea.

"Please tell me High Brother Luc is going with you," DiCook said.

I nodded.

His shoulders relaxed a fraction. "Good. He'll keep you from doing something stupid."

"I need to trust you to keep Yanaba safe," I said quietly.

DiCook frowned at me. "You're taking both Little Bear and Gina with you?"

"No, of course not." I shook my head.

"But they're training the entire squad of wardens who will be accompanying Elizabeth to the Duchy of Anacapa." He gestured wildly. "Why do I need to keep an eye on your junior justice?"

I chuckled. "Malven, what did she do when I went to Tandor last winter?"

"She wasn't stupid enough to leave her body while you were in Diné in the fall," he pointed out.

"But now she has a son to guard as well as performing her Temple duties." I refilled my cup before I offered DiCook more wine. He held up his hand to politely decline anymore.

"I will do my best to protect and counsel Justice Yanaba, Chief Justice." He raised his cup in salute. "However, I ask in return that first of all, you do not get yourself killed and secondly, you come home."

I returned his salute. "I can't guarantee the first one, but if I'm alive, I definitely won't stay in Jing."

"And last of all, would Justice Yanaba be open to continue meeting for the midday meal on First Day to revue the city's legal matters?" His hopeful expression made me laugh.

"I promise to make arrangements, my dear Magistrate," I said. "I would hate for you to waste away from the lack of decent food before I return."

"Your consideration is much appreciated." DiCook inclined his head.

During the rest of the meal, we discussed matters of security for the city of Orrin for the next few months.

Thankfully, Luc's visit shortly after Second Evening stopped Sivan's tirade over my lack of formal wear for a state visit. She was pleased I was taking a portion of my Mill gold with me.

"Maybe the Jing Balance staff can assist in dressing you appropriately," Sivan snapped.

"I'm sure Sister Shi Hua and Mistress Yin Li will make sure I don't enter the imperial palace in rags," I answered as I gently guided my head of household out of my bedchambers.

Luc's humor tickled the back of my mind while I locked the door behind Sivan.

"Do I need to ward my rooms?" I asked.

He crossed to my bed, sat, and laid his crutches on the floor beside the footboard. "If it's any consolation, I got a similar lecture from Istaqa."

I crossed my arms. "In other words, I do need to raise a ward so neither of our heads of households burst in to continue lecturing us." I whispered the words and made the requisite gestures. Balance magic always felt solid to me. A physical presence.

"It could be worse," Luc grumbled when I finished.

I winced. "Shi Hua isn't taking this journey very well, is she?"

"None of us expected this." Luc scrubbed his face before his attention returned to me. "We already found a wet nurse to supplement Chao's meals, which helps. However, Jeremy's heart-broken and scared of raising the babe by himself over the next four years. Mateqai is snapping at everyone. Poor Garbhan's attempting to keep the peace, but he's terrified how Reverend Father Farrell will react when he learns I've left Issura."

He exhaled heavily. "Thank you for speaking to Leocadia and Dragonfly on my behalf."

I crossed to my bed and sat beside him. "You're welcome. However, I can't take all the credit. Both ladies realize the Issuran Temples need to change our ways before the demons slaughter us all."

"That's part of what worries me," Luc murmured.

"Really?" A bark of laughter erupted from me. "We're going to another nation where the nobility actively dislikes their new emperor. They and others will accuse said new emperor of engineering the demon attack that killed his brother and nephews. We're doing this without the permission from the heads of our own Temples, and the queen who issued the order to us has plausible deniability if we survive long enough to return to Issura."

"You are truly a bowl-is-half-empty woman, aren't you?" Luc said dryly.

"You forgot the bowl also spills before I can take a spoonful," I added.

"Quan needs us." Luc threaded the fingers of his right hand through the fingers of my left. "And we do owe him."

"I know." I sighed. "I just wish we didn't have to rip apart Shi Hua's spirit in the process."

Chapter 10

My stomach still bothered me the next morning. I wasn't sure if it were nerves about our journey, or if I'd developed an ailment. Sivan laid the back of her hand on my forehead as I bathed.

"You're not fevered, m'lady." She frowned. "It may be your body's reaction to everything you've been through over the past year."

"But I've gone to all my sessions with High Sister Mya," I protested.

"So has Brother Jeremy," Sivan chided. "And Ming Wei. And High Brother Luc and Sister Claudia. The damage to one's spirit isn't as easily seen as the damage to one's body. And the spiritual damage acts as an infection if it's not dealt with immediately."

But there seemed to be more underlying her words that Sivan wasn't saying.

"Tell me truly what you are thinking." I gazed at her. "I don't want anything unspoken between us for the months I will be gone."

She sighed and perched on the stool by the bathing pool. "I ask that this stays between us, m'lady."

"Of course."

"I know you and High Brother Talbert suspect something is wrong with Reverend Mother Alara, but it may not be senility or sympathy for the renegades." Sivan twined her fingers together and stared at them for a moment before her attention returned to me. "It's more of an issue of raising children. Or the lack of ability to raise them. In some ways, the Reverend Mother treated you far more poorly than Gerd."

Her observation surprised me. "I wasn't exactly the best novice at the home Temple."

Sivan pursed her lips before she added, "Elizabeth told me some of what happened to you when you were a novice. And I have seen the lash scars on your back. How is that any different than what was done to Ming Wei? Between Gerd and the Reverend Mother, you already had spiritual injuries the demons exploited. And now that Mya is working with you, the infection from all of the old emotional injuries are draining, and the purulence has to go somewhere. Given your normal appetite, and the fact you're not showing any other symptoms, I fear your digestive issues may be a symptom of your emotional scars."

That was the longest speech from Sivan that didn't involve her irritation with my clothing or hair.

"Thank you for your honesty," I murmured.

"Now's when you'd threaten me with a lashing for impertinence," she said dryly.

"Normally, yes, but that's after I've warned you to be silent." I smiled. "I'm going to miss your wise counsel over the next few months."

"Just come home alive, Anthea," she said softly.

Our party couldn't avoid notice from the citizens of Orrin when we headed down to the docks a candlemark before First Afternoon. Not in the middle of winter with the fishwives whispering about the provisioning of the duke's flagship. Crowds of shop keepers, craftspeople, and their customers muttered among themselves, especially since the man they knew as Ambassador Quan was with us. So there was a lot of conjecture among the civilians as to what was going on.

Duke Marco, Lady Katarina, and their entourage were already at the *Mars Tranquilus*'s berth when we arrived. The nobleman appeared worried, but his wife's skin glowed red with anger, and she clutched little Kam tightly in her arms. I dismounted and approached the couple while Little Bear and Hogarth supervised the transfer of our gear from the Temple cart onto the ship.

I inclined my head to Marco. "Thank you for the use of the *Mars Tranquilus* and her crew, Your Grace."

"Stay here, Anthea," Katarina hissed under her breath. "No good will come from two Issuran seats accompanying the Jing ambassador home."

This was why I hated juggling everyone's secrets. The DiMaras knew Quan was related to the former Jing emperor, but they didn't know Quan was now the heir to the throne. Nor could I tell them how important this voyage was, and mine and Luc's presence at Quan's coronation were ordered by Queen Teodora herself.

"It's necessary," I murmured. "When we get home, I'll explain everything to you both. I promise."

Luc approached and smiled at the couple. "Keep our godson out of trouble while we gone." He kissed the top of the babe's head. "May the Lord of Light watch over you and protect you, Kam."

I smiled. "He'll be walking before we return home."

"And you should be here to see him take his first steps." There was a catch in Katarina's voice, and she blinked rapidly to keep from shedding tears. Her efforts didn't succeed. Fat yellow drops rolled down to splash on her son's delicate skin.

"We'll be back as soon as we can," I whispered. "Be well, little one." I kissed Kam's forehead as well.

He laughed and waved his chubby arms. I was going to miss him terribly.

I was going to miss everyone in Orrin terribly.

"We'll be back in a few months." I kissed Katarina on her damp cheek though she refused to look at me. I shifted and hugged Marco, and he returned the gesture fiercely.

"Don't get yourself killed, Anthea," he whispered in my ear.

"I won't," I whispered back.

He released me reluctantly. I turned away, and Little Bear escorted me down the pier to board the *Mars Tranquilus*. I didn't look back because if I did, I would start crying, too.

Chapter 11

❖

The *Mars Tranquilus* wasn't as roomy as Reverend Father Biming's ship the *Unbridled*. But then, the *Mars Tranquilus* wasn't expected to sail around the world either. I wasn't thrilled about dashing across the Peaceful Sea in the middle of winter in any ship, but Captain Titus had an excellent weather oracle as part of his crew. A weather wizard would have been preferable, but they were almost as rare as sighted justices.

Quan tried to offer his services as a sailor to Titus, but his overture was immediately nixed by all the Temple personnel before Titus had a chance to say no. As Sister Shi Hua lectured, she wasn't about to lose the crown prince of Jing to a broken line or a rogue wave.

Titus graciously turned over his cabin to his guests from Jing. The Issuran contingent took the passenger cabin.

I was rather glad Luc selected Warden Yar to accompany him. Little Yin Shang, Yin Li's son, absolutely adored the gentle giant. The boy viewed the voyage as a grand adventure. Yar kept Yin Shang amused, and more importantly, out of the way of the crew.

The crimson sun was directly overhead when the Temple bells rang First Afternoon. Titus bellowed orders, and the crew raised the sails. The sailors carefully tacked the *Mars Tranquilus* toward the harbor entrance.

Leaning my forearms on the forward rail and staying well out of the way of the crew, I shivered as we approached the rocks on the north end of the bay. It reminded me too much of my half-brother Bumblebee and I taking a proverbial leap of faith off the cliffs of Tandor's own bay as the clergy of Death launched their last resort spells.

Somehow, we both managed to land in the water rather than on top of the sea-washed stones at the base of the cliff. Mya was the only person I ever told of my vision of Balance ordering us to jump. "Vision" was a rather loose word for the experience. Since I didn't see the way sighted humans did, She wasn't like how the statues of Her felt or looked. Balance had been a pillar of blinding white light, and Her voice had sounded familiar.

Which was odd since I'd never had one of the Twelve speak to me before the Siege of Tandor.

But within moments, the *Mars Tranquilus* cleared the Bay of Orrin, and we sailed southward on the open sea. Gulls circled overhead, following in hopes of food. They would have better luck during clamming season on Sandy Spit.

"May I join you, Chief Justice?" Quan stepped up to the rail beside me.

"Of course, Your Highness." We both stared at the horizon. Or rather he did. The weather was supposed to remain clear for the next two days, which meant it was difficult for me to tell the difference between the sea and sky. However, my strange sight could detect differences in the heat of clouds long before a potential storm reached me.

"What?" he murmured in mock dismay. "No lecture on caution because I need to reach Jing alive?"

I shrugged. "If you're asking me to toss you overboard, you should have done so on our trip to Tandor. I might have obliged you then."

Quan turned to face me. "May I ask your advice about a personal matter?"

I looked up at him. "That depends. Will my wardens want to defend my honor regarding such a personal matter?"

His mouth pursed for a moment before he said, "This is more a question of state, and I would like a friend's opinion."

"Oh." I was a little surprised he considered me a friend, but after the last year and a half, I supposed we'd developed a rapport. "Then yes, you may ask."

"What is your opinion of Sister Shi Hua?"

I cocked my head. "I beg your pardon?"

"I am being serious in asking," he said crossly.

"Except your tone sounded more like a suitor jealous of his rival," I said lightly.

"I wanted to petition the Temple of Light to release her from her vows and allow her to marry me," Quan said softly.

Several responses ran through my mind, but I settled on, "May I ask why?"

"Now, who sounds like a jealous suitor?" Quan teased. He sighed when I didn't respond. "Because she's a Light talent and I'm not. Because we already know she's fertile thanks to Brother Jeremy. And because she's one of the few people I trust."

I had to give Quan credit. He'd thought this matter through, but I wasn't sure of one last thing. "I cannot fault your logic except for one thing. Why are you asking me, and not Yin Li or Shi Hua herself?"

His jaw muscles twitched, which sent the gold beads weighting the ends of his moustache swinging. "I did speak with Yin Li about the matter. She also said she agreed with my reasoning, but she couldn't speak for her niece. She suggested I seek your counsel because you know the woman Shi Hua has become better than she knew the child Shi Hua was."

Surprise wasn't exactly the emotion swirling through me. If Shi Hua were empress, she'd know how to protect herself and her children as well as protect Quan. But would Light Warden Mateqai come home with us? He'd become rather attached to the young priestess, even laying down his life for her, though his feelings weren't anything like romantic love. On the other hand, Shi Hua could use someone she could trust, too.

"You do realize you'll probably inherit Warden Mateqai if she accepts your proposal, don't you?" I said wryly. "You might want to discuss this with the high brother before you steal away one of his wardens. He's already vexed about losing Shi Hua."

"Hmmm." Quan stroked his beard. "I'd rather hoped you would speak to the high brother. I fear he'd gut me before I even said the sister's name on the assumption I meant to propose to you."

I roared with laughter and slapped the railing.

"What is so humorous?" Luc asked as he approached.

"I'll only tell if you promise to keep your steel sheathed," I teased.

He glared at Quan. "What did you do this time?"

"Propriety, High Brother," the prince chided. "The correct phrasing is 'what did you do this time, Your Highness.'"

"Don't make me irritate the chief justice by unsheathing my weapon," Luc growled.

"Can we please not spend the entire journey with your two waving your unsheathed weapons at each other?" I snapped.

"The chief justice speaks wisely since I need your counsel, High Brother," Quan said.

Luc leaned back with a shocked expression. "You do, Your Highness?"

Once again, Quan laid out his reasons for wanting to marry Shi Hua. "How do I approach my own Reverend Father of Light with this proposal?"

From the tickle of Luc's emotions, he was seriously contemplating Quan's question. "Let us retreat to a more important question. What has Shi Hua said about this plan?"

Quan grunted. "Why is everyone obsessed with what she says?"

Luc and I exchanged looks before I cleared my throat. "You do know she prefers women, don't you? The only reason she laid with anyone, including Brother Jeremy, was because of the breeding edict."

"I am well aware I would not be her first choice of bed partners if she were released from her Temple vows," Quan said dryly. "I planned to offer her the services of my concubines, or have a priestess from Love entertain her."

"And if you need some assistance from another woman in your bed to ensure conception, you won't object to that either," I teased.

Quan bestowed one of his lascivious smiles upon me. "Are you volunteering, my dear Chief Justice?"

"No, she isn't," Luc snapped.

"Or I could request the Temple of Balance to release you from your vows?" he continued. "Then Shi Hua would simply be your surrogate."

"You will do no such thing!" Luc yelled.

I glared at him. I thought we both had made progress on our jealousy issues through the aid of Child. But apparently, one of us had not grown as much as the other.

"I do not believe it is your decision to make, High Brother," I chided gently.

He snorted and swung off on his crutches in a snit.

"I apologize, Anthea," Quan murmured. "I didn't think Luc would take my jests as seriously as he used to with the ongoing edict."

I sighed. "It's not you, Po." If he was going to use my given name, I would do the same regardless of our respective statuses. Deep down, I'd become fond of him, though there would never be anything more between us. "This has more to do with the loss of his child."

Quan's mien turned even more solemn. "Such a loss is never easy. My brother's wife was pregnant with their third child."

His news hit me like a blow to the abdomen. Like Luc's son, Quan's nephew never even had the opportunity to take his first breath.

"I grieve with you." The formal ritual words of the Temple of Death seemed so inadequate at the moment.

Quan nodded briefly. "I shall go make amends with the high brother. This voyage will be difficult enough without his hands about my throat."

"That's an excellent idea," I said.

He turned away from the rail to embark on his task when I added, "And Po?"

Quan looked at me with a raised eyebrow.

"Neither of your scenarios involving me is ever going to happen."

He laughed. "We'll see."

Chapter 12

We sailed southeast for a few days before the sails of the *Mars Tranquilus* caught the easterly trade winds. Captain Titus believed if the winds held we might arrive at the Kingdom of Ryukyu a week early. I would be perfectly happy with an uneventful voyage. However, I never said a word out loud for fear the Twelve would decide to teach me yet another lesson.

Tensions eased among the passengers and crew aboard the ship as we settled into the two-month voyage. Two whole months without having to fear any demon attacks. For some reason we humans had yet to discern, demons disliked water. They didn't seem to be able to swim, and they were equally adverse to salt and fresh water. There were reports of demons sacrificing themselves by lying in a creek or small river bed to create a bridge for their fellows. But a ship at sea was relatively safe for us humans.

Unless someone was idiotic enough to summon a demon on a ship at sea.

The only real issue amongst the crew and passengers was Shi Hua's despondency over leaving her son behind. I couldn't blame her. She actually loved Chao, and she'd expected to spend his early years with him until he had to go to the home Temple of Light in Standora for his training.

At least, her distance speaking talent brought her a slight measure of comfort with Jeremy's daily status reports as to Chao's health and well-being. Oftentimes, Yanaba, Elizabeth, or Talbert would join in the link regarding Temple business or issues within the city. Our fellow clergy were all rather amused by the politely nasty responses they received from the Reverend Mother of Balance and the Reverend Father of Light. However, true to her word, the queen bluntly told them she had given Luc and me a standing order to assist Crown Prince Quan Po of Jing should the need arise after he'd given so much aid to Issura over the years.

Also once a week, Shi Hua facilitated conversations between the Issuran passengers and crew with their loved ones back home. That bought her a lot of favor from Titus and his sailors. And Reverend Father Biming gave regular updates on the status of the empire to Quan.

The only real issue for everyone aboard the ship was the damn cold at night. On board a ship, open flames were a danger to everyone, so we didn't dare have braziers in our cabins. The winter winds blew constantly which sped our voyage, but it cut through the layers of cotton, silk, leather, wool, and fur I wore and brought out regular gooseflesh on my skin.

I slept with Luc in his bed, not for entertainment, but to keep warm during the long winter nights. Our wardens did the same in their extra large hammocks. Sometime, little Yin Shang traded with Mateqai, so the boy slept with Yar, and the warden with Shi Hua.

Mateqai joked he preferred sleeping with Yar, too. The body heat of the giant warden from the Old Continent steppes was better than any warming pan.

I was glad I had Donella copy some scrolls from Knowledge's library I wished to read. We lost the Balance library thanks to Yanaba, but I couldn't blame the young justice. Destroying the demons within Orrin last spring was worth the loss of our records and books as well as my worn clothing.

Midafternoon on Second Day of the third week of our trip, Luc attempted to meditate by sitting cross-legged on the cabin deck despite the rolling motion of the ship while I read in our bed, my back supported by the wall. At the cabin's table, Wardens Jonata and Long Feather played a Jing game with thick paper circles called Leaf.

The knock on the door echoed through the cabin despite the moan of the wind outside. Long Feather rose from his bench. I found it amusing the sailors nailed their furniture to the deck, but it made sense. The last thing passengers or crew needed was furniture flying about in rough weather.

Even with being on the ship alone for two weeks, Long Feather kept his hand on his knife. He opened the cabin door and bowed. "Greetings, Sister Shi Hua."

The Jing priestess stalked into our cabin. "May I please speak with the chief justice and the high brother alone?"

Long Feather and Jonata exchanged looks before they both turned to me. From Shi Hua's agitation grating along my psyche, I had a pretty good idea what concerned her. I nodded to my wardens. Jonata collected the paper circles and placed them in their oiled leather bag before both wardens departed.

I set aside my scroll, crawled off the bed, and helped Luc up from the deck. We sat on the bench Jonata had abandoned while Shi Hua perched on the opposing side.

"Did news come from Jing or Issura?" I asked.

"You could say that," she snapped. "The crown prince just asked me to marry him. Not because he loves me, but to make sure he has an heir because I proved my fertility."

Oh, Balance! If that was how he worded his proposal, no wonder she was offended.

Luc leaned close to my right ear and muttered, "I told you he'd make a farce of this."

I glared at him. "Maybe you need to leave, too."

"Oh, Light." Shi Hua groaned. "You both knew he planned to do this and you didn't warn me?"

"He did ask our advice on the concept," I said. "But we both told him he needed to talk to you about his idea."

She stared at me. "You encouraged him?"

"Yin Li is the one who told him he should court you properly," Luc protested.

"My aunt was in on this, too?" Shi Hua's coloring shifted into a darker red than I thought humanly possible.

I shrugged. "A good leader seeks counsel. It is a very logical plan given the political circumstance in Chengzhou right now."

"Doesn't anyone care what I want?" Shi Hua cried out.

"When have any of us gotten what we want in life?" I grabbed her hands. "You have the opportunity to leave Temple life. That's freedom. Do you really want to say no to Quan?"

"I already had to give up one child," she snapped as she jerked her hand away from me. "Marrying him means all of my children will have targets on them. How is that freedom?"

"Did he tell you what he was willing to offer you?" Luc asked.

"It doesn't matter!" she shrieked.

I exchanged a look with Luc. There was definitely something we were missing here.

"What exactly did Quan say to you?" I asked gently.

"That it was in the best interest of Jing for him to marry a Light priestess given his Thief talent, and I was the best choice because neither of us would have romantic feelings for the other." Her huff at the end indicated how insulted she was.

I rubbed the bridge of my nose. For such a smooth talker, Quan could be a total idiot at times.

When I lowered my hand, I decided a different tactic was needed. "Do you have romantic feelings for Warden Mateqai?"

"What? No!" she protested.

"Do you believe he has romantic feelings for you?" I asked.

Surprisingly, she took a long moment to consider my question. "I do not believe so. But what does that have to do with anything?"

"Is it correct to say you each do your duties to the best of your abilities and you respect the other person's skills to do the same?" I continued.

"It's a little more than that," she quietly admitted. "I would consider him a friend as well as a colleague." At least, she was calming down and listening to me.

"Has it occurred to you that you would be Quan's Mateqai?"

"No, it hasn't," she conceded.

"You have served Quan for seven, going on eight, years, Shi Hua," I said softly. "Has he ever disrespected you?"

"No," she reluctantly admitted.

"Has he ever made you question his motives?"

A tiny smirk twisted her mouth. "Only when it came to his pursuit of you."

"He needs a friend who can watch his back, which is exactly what Reverend Father Biming trained you for." I sighed. "Maybe the Reverend Father never expected Quan to ask you to marry him. But then again, I personally wouldn't put it past Biming either because no matter how much he loves Quan, Biming cannot bear him any children."

My last comment made Shi Hua giggle. Sometimes, I forgot just how young she was.

"All right," she finally said. "I'll talk to him, but Anthea, I want you to negotiate my marriage contract for me."

I smiled. "It would be my honor, Your Highness."

Chapter 13

The negotiations for the marital contract between Quan and Shi Hua kept Luc and me busy for the next couple of weeks of the voyage. Half the crew and passengers were giving both parties their two coppers on what the couple should negotiate for. The other half were wagering whether or not the wedding would actually happen.

Neither group was helping the situation one bit.

It was so hard to hide anything on this ship. I wondered how in the Twelve Titus's predecessor Arturo managed to get a demon egg on board without everyone knowing about it.

For the duration of the negotiations, Shi Hua slept with me in the passenger cabin. Luc stayed in the captain's cabin. He ended up sharing a bed with Mateqai after the two Light wardens tossed dice to decide who stayed with their high brother.

I would have joined in with Captain Titus's laughter at the ludicrousness of the whole situation if the political stability of the entire Peaceful Sea wasn't riding on the success of this nuptial contract.

Every nation on the rim depended on trade for raw materials, especially for necessities like Jing flash powder and iron ore now that the demons had renewed their assaults. None of us could afford to lose Jing. If a civil war erupted, the populace of Jing would be easy pickings for a demon army.

Including the one we suspected was waiting out in the Gobi Desert north and west of Jing.

"Anthea?"

I jerked at Luc saying my name. "I'm sorry. What did you say about the annual stipend should the marriage terminate?"

We sat on the floor in an empty storage room on the second deck since there wasn't time to fully load the *Mars Tranquilus* with trade goods. Titus didn't want a full cargo anyway, not with the possibility of nasty winter storms that might cause us to founder. Everyone on board assumed Luc and I were avoiding any appearance of favoritism by using the captain's and passenger cabins, but the storage room was the only place where we could get any privacy.

"You were a million leagues away," he said with a concerned expression. "What's wrong?"

"I can't escape the feeling the demons we suspect are hiding in the Gobi Desert did capture Reverend Father Chen and his troops," I said in a rush. "The renegades tortured the information out of Chen's people because those demons knew exactly how to get into the imperial palace. And I think the attacks were a test, not the actual offensive."

Luc exhaled and leaned back against the bare wall. "You're not the only one who's been thinking about it."

"You, too?" Relief spread through me. High Sister Mya had been working with me about my obsessive need to analyze and be correct in my logic.

"Quan and Yin Li brought up the idea individually to me before I mentioned my own thoughts." Luc cocked his head. "But there's another possibility. Perhaps the emperor did not eliminate everyone within the palace who had renegade sympathies."

I relaxed against the opposing wall while I ran through the possibilities. "Chengwu's own father or any one else from the School of Sorcery with palace access could have delivered the information to the renegades before the crackdown."

"True." Luc sighed. "It's easier to change personnel than changing the very walls of the imperial palace."

"Unless Chengzhou has a tunnel system similar to Issuran cities," I said. "I think we need to finish today's negotiation points later and talk to Quan, Yin Li, and Shi Hua."

We packed our notes and writing instruments into our documents bags. I stood and held out a hand to Luc.

He slung his bag strap across his body before he grasped my hand, and I pulled him to his foot. He grabbed his crutches and extinguished his light ball.

"Sometimes, I envy you," he said as we made our way to the ladder at the fore hatch.

"Why? I wouldn't wish my life on anyone," I protested.

He handed me his crutches and placed his hands on the rung level with his head. "If we all had your type of sight this whole war would be over much faster."

I chuckled. "That doesn't exactly solve our issues with human stupidity."

He climbed using a hopping maneuver and the strength of his arms. Anguish swept through me. What if one of the rungs broke and he fell? What would he do decades down the road when his arms would no longer support his weight?

When he reached the top of the ladder, Yar was there to assist him to through the hatch. I held up the crutches, and Yar grabbed them and gave them to Luc. I scrambled up the ladder and tried to focus on our more immediate issue, instead of my fears for the future.

I collected Shi Hua from the passenger cabin while Luc found Quan with Titus on the bridge. The only person happy with our appearance was Yin Shang who got out of his afternoon lessons with his mother. The little boy ran out of the captain's quarters to find Yar.

The Love priestess smiled. "Does this mean we've come to an agreement on the marital contract?"

Luc and I looked at each other before I said, "No. We may have another problem."

Once Luc and I laid out our discussion in the storage room, I added, "I don't want to hear you've been assassinated as soon as the *Mars Tranquilus* leaves Jing."

"Why, Anthea, you almost sound like you care for my well-being." Despite his attempt at levity, an underlying burr in his voice indicated how disturbed he was.

"There are tunnels between the Temples in Chengzhou," Yin Li said. "All of the major Jing cities and a few of the mid-sized towns with the full presence of the Twelve have them."

"But there's not a tunnel directly between the Temples and the imperial palace," Shi Hua said. "Should the palace or the Temples fall, there's no way for the enemy to get into the other without a battle."

"What about other secret entrances to the palace?" I asked.

From the odd looks the three people from Jing gave each other, I knew how the demons got into the palace.

"Supposedly only Thief and the imperial bodyguards from the Temples know about the ways into the palace," Shi Hua said. "But the entrances are sealed by magic like the ones in the Issuran Temples. If those spells are not deactivated correctly, the alarms will go off."

"Then someone gave the demons the key to opening them," Luc said. "Would anyone with Reverend Father Chen know about these entrances?"

Yin Li's face turned a sickly greenish-yellow. "Yes. The Reverend Father Chen and High Brother Shang." Her son's father. No wonder she was distraught.

"Or there's another possibility," Quan said.

We all looked at him expectantly. For the first time since I'd met him, fright flowed from him along with worry and rage.

"There's an exit known only to whoever holds the imperial throne and their children," he said grimly. "There are more conventional booby-traps, but no magical seal. No alarm would sound if someone came in that way. Not even Reverend Father Biming knows about it."

All I could do was stare at him. His brother may have died because of one unsecured exit.

Chapter 14

Before Luc or I could say a word, Shi Hua leapt to her feet. "Would you have even told me about it? Or would you leave me behind to be slaughtered by the demons?"

"I don't know if it's still there," he snapped. "It's entirely likely our late emperor may have disabled it because his father knew about it, and that's the reason my brother and my nephews died!"

I lowered my voice an octave. "There's nothing to be accomplished by shouting at each other."

"I'm—I'm—" Shi Hua clenched her fists. "I'm so tired of all these damn secrets!" She burst out crying.

Yin Li scrambled across the cabin to sit next to Shi Hua on the built-in bed. She pulled the younger priestess into her arms and rocked her while murmuring soothing words in the Jing language.

"I agree with you, Shi Hua." I pushed to my feet while I glared at Quan. "You claim you want a true partnership with my patron in these nuptial negotiations. You need to speak with Brother Luc and decide if you wish to continue. Because if you're not more forthcoming with pertinent information, we are done."

I marched over to Shi Hua, and with Yin Li's assistance, we helped her out of the captain's cabin.

Once the poor Light priestess had cried herself to sleep, Yin Li motioned for me to follow her. Mateqai took a stance in front of the passenger cabin door. No one would disturb Shi Hua.

Yin Li and I walked to the bow of the ship for the semblance of a private conversation. Warden Jonata and one of the Jing guards stood nearby to enforce that illusion of privacy. Sea birds had stopped following us weeks ago, so the only sounds were the creak of the ship and the whistle of the wind through the rigging and past the sails.

"I am worried about my niece," Yin Li murmured.

"As am I." I sighed and leaned my elbows on the railing. "I know Quan has his own secrets to protect, but I never dreamed he'd manipulate Shi Hua to this extent. I have to agree with her. There are too many damn secrets in our world, and it's getting people killed."

"There are secrets, that if released, will condemn more to Death's embrace," Yin Li said.

I understood her position as the Jing crown prince's current bodyguard, but I blindly assumed she would be concerned about her niece's welfare as well. The wind rippled the edges of my hood and tossed the hem of my cloak this way and that as I considered my next words.

"Since you have experience in childbirth, how much of her anguish is caused by her body readjusting to its original state?" I asked.

"I am sure that is part of the problem," Yin Li said. "The other is that we both have ten years on her. Until last year, her biggest challenge was to keep Po alive." The sadness in her voice made me realize that Quan wasn't the only one grieving.

"You would be dead, too, if you had been at Emperor Chengwu's side," I said.

"Do you really believe that helps, Chief Justice?" she asked bitterly.

"No, but I need you to think logically instead of wallowing in your grief," I snapped. "Otherwise, we will lose both Quan and Shi Hua."

She frowned at me. "Why are you so adamant about this marriage despite your threat to him?"

"Because they need each other." At Yin Li's odd expression, I slashed my hand through the air. "I don't mean in a carnal manner. They actually like and respect each other. They each have skills that complement the other's talents. They—"

"Need to keep Jing stable so Issura can continue making money from the trade routes," Yin Li said dryly.

"If Jing falls, how long do you think the rest of us will be able to hold up against the demons?" I murmured. "Have you asked Shi Hua about what happened in Tandor?"

Yin Li's anger dropped away. "She refuses to speak about it."

"So does Chao's father," I said softly. "Brother Jeremy had to go to Child to deal with the nightmares. In fact, High Sister Mya and her people have been so busy since the fall of Tandor, she had to ask the home Temple in Standora for some extra clergy to deal with the large amount of clergy and citizens needing Child's assistance."

Yin Li clutched the railing and resumed staring at the ocean. "She never said a word about how bad it was." She shook her head. "I told my sister I would look out for her when she started exhibiting Light talent and was sent to Chengzhou for training. I was a fool to promise such a thing."

"To paraphrase your own words to Quan, you kept your promise to your sister by looking out for the child your niece was." I rested my left hand on top of Yin Li's right hand. "But she is a woman now, and she needs to make her own decisions."

Yin Li looked at me again. "You speak wise words, Anthea, but I fear you are placing your own desires to escape Temple service upon my niece."

I laughed long and loud while she favored me with a puzzled expression.

Finally, she asked, "Are you going to share what's so amusing with me?"

"Quan already tried to propose to me, and I said no."

Chapter 15

In hindsight, my confession to Yin Li probably was not one of my most intelligent acts. I wasn't sure if she were furious with me for declining Po's suggestion, or if she were enraged her beloved niece was the crown prince's second choice. The angry Love priestess stomped to the midship section and loudly insisted my warden Long Father needed to share Quan's bed, and she would sleep with Jonata. Both of my wardens stared at me with concerned expressions when I caught up with Yin Li.

I rubbed my forehead. "We will accommodate Mistress Yin Li's wishes." I turned and glared at her. "For tonight only."

"Uh, Chief Justice, am I . . ." Long Feather's eyes looked everywhere but at me. It was Quan's own damn fault for his reputation in regards to bed partners.

"You are sharing a bed for sleeping with someone in the captain's cabin," I said wearily. "I don't care who. And if anybody, Jing or Issuran, insists on bedplay with you, tell them they need my permission first, and I will behead them for you to make it clear they will never have such permission."

Long Feather pursed his lips together for a long moment before he tightly said, "Yes, m'lady."

My dark sense of humor was not helping this situation.

I wanted off the *Mars Tranquilus*. I wanted a very hot bath. And I wanted a pot of Jing tea. Only one of which I could obtain at the moment.

I stalked across the main deck and climbed the steps to the quarterdeck. Captain Titus had command of the ship's wheel. He wore a slight smirk his blue-green facial hair did not cover, which meant he'd heard the exchange with Yin Li and my wardens. However, he remained silent.

"No comments this time, Captain?" I muttered.

"None whatsoever, Chief Justice," he said agreeably.

"Really?" I rested my hands on the deck railing to keep my balance. The wind had picked up, but First Officer Iniki, the ship's weather oracle, had warned everyone the night before that a storm passed to the north of us and both air and sea would be ruffled today because of it.

I didn't question the oracle's accuracy. I could see greens and yellows swirl with blues and purples near the northwest horizon, a sure sign of a tempest we didn't want to be in.

On the other hand, the skies south of us were a clear dark blue—

"What's wrong, m'lady?" Titus asked.

"Something's moving near the west by southwest horizon," I answered. The object was barely discernable between the sea and sky, but it was a lighter blue than both.

The captain frowned. "It's too early in the season for the humpback pods to be migrating north."

I crossed to the opposite side of the quarterdeck and peered in the distance. "We haven't seen any other ships, have we?"

"No, m'lady," he answered. "Not since we passed the Anacapa Islands. We're the only one mad enough to cross the northern Peaceful Sea before midwinter. Not even the Sea Peoples are sailing this far north yet."

"Then we may have a problem."

"Sea Wolf, take the wheel!" Titus called out.

"Aye, Captain!" The sailor scrambled up the stairs to the quarterdeck and took control of the rudder. Like Titus, he was tall with broad shoulders from his western Old Continent ancestry, but he wore his hair uncut in the Chumash style and shunned the facial hair that had become a fashion statement in Issura.

Titus pulled out a distance-viewer from his case of navigation equipment. He looked in the direction I named. His frown deepened.

"Little Squirrel!"

"Aye, sir! The second officer ran up the steps. She was a small, wiry woman who kept her hair cut close to her scalp, but she was just as strong as any of her male colleagues.

"There's an object thirty degrees off the port bow." Titus handed her a second distance-viewer with a long strap. "Give me a report."

"Aye, sir!" Little Squirrel slung the leather strap over her body and raced back down the stairs. She scrambled up the main mast just like her namesake, finding hand and footholds I couldn't detect until she reached the tiny enclosed spot the sailors referred to as a crow's nest.

"Captain Titus, may I borrow your distance-viewer?" I asked.

He handed it to me without any objection.

I peered in the direction of the strange object. There was a thin line of yellow below the object. Just like the line of yellow around the *Mars Tranquilus* caused by the high displacement of water by the ship's speed. I spotted another thin blur of pale yellow behind it.

"There's two ships," I murmured and handed the distance viewer back to Titus.

"Captain!" Little Squirrel yelled from the yardarm of the main mast. "Three ships on an intercept course!"

Everyone topside, both passengers and sailors, froze in place.

"Type and colors!" he called back.

"No colors!" Little Squirrel checked the distance-viewer again. "Captain, they look like langskips!" There was a puzzled note in her voice.

"Langskips?" I asked.

"They are the ships used by the Skandza a couple of centuries ago," Titus said, but his attention was on the horizon.

"The Skandza Territories are on the other side of the Old Continent," I blurted.

"And they've stopped using langskips for ocean travel. A caravel is faster and has more cargo space." He raised his voice to a bellow. "Little Squirrel, get down here! All Hands! General quarters! Secure for evasive maneuvers!"

Sailors raced around the deck, tying down things and stowing loose equipment.

"What can we do to help, Captain?" I asked. Most of the passengers outranked him on land, but this ship was his domain.

"Get the passengers in their cabins, Chief Justice," Titus said. "And pray to the Twelve, we can get out of this."

Chapter 16

I raced down the steps and around the banister at the same time Luc burst out of the captain's cabin.

"What's going on?" he demanded.

"Three ships on a course to intercept us." I turned and did some bellowing of my own. "Passengers, to your cabins." I repeated the phrase in Jing.

Or I thought I did. I could have accidentally claimed I just laid an egg. However, the non-sailors on the main deck of both nations responded to my commands.

Mateqai ran up to us, followed by Yar and a couple of the Jing guards. "What do we need to do, Chief Justice?"

With a start, I realized I was the senior clergy on board. I had become a seat a month before Luc officially replaced Kam.

"Get in your cabins. Arm yourselves." I sucked in a deep breath. "And pray to the Twelve, Titus and his crew can outsail whoever is after us."

For some strange reason, we all collected ourselves in the captain's quarters. It was more for the comfort in shared danger than any defensive plan. Everyone was armed. Even little Yin Shang had a knife. Yin Li tried to hold him, but he insisted on sitting next to Yar with a fierce expression on his round face.

"I hate waiting," Quan growled.

I really wanted to agree with him, but I couldn't. Not when so many lives depended on me keeping my composure.

"There's nothing Captain Titus and his crew cannot handle when it comes to the *Mars Tranquilus*," I said sternly. "We all will be in the way on the decks. If we get boarded, then we help defend the ship, but you, my dear Prince, will stay in here with your bodyguards." Shi Hua was translating for the two guards who had accompanied Yin Li to Issura last summer since their Issuran wasn't as fluent as the rest of the Jing contingent.

"We will defend the prince with our lives," Yin Shang said. His statement was as fierce as his expression.

Even though nearly everyone else had to swallow their laughter, I nodded solemnly. "I trust you to keep the prince alive, good sir."

"I come to serve." He inclined his head with his formal response. Up on one of the beds, Yin Li wiped the tears from her eyes. She had already lost the boy's father. Now, her son was growing up faster than his winter age warranted.

"Your service honors us." Despite my traditional response, I added sternly, "However, your mother is the senior rank in the prince's defense. You will obey her orders. Please do not force me to try and punish you for insubordination, Yin Shang."

His eyes widened. "I understand, and I will obey my superior to the best of my ability, Lady Justice."

I sighed. "Thank you, good sir."

And we continued our wait.

Timbers and ropes creaked, and sails snapped. Titus called out orders, but the exact words were muffled.

Without the Temple bells to call time and not being able to see the sun, I wasn't sure how long we sat in the captain's quarters. We took turns walking and stretching in the close confines in order to stay limber if a battle were in our future. But the ship's pitching and rolling made even that more difficult.

A knock on the door made us all jump. Little Squirrel opened the door and stuck her head around the jamb. "The captain wants your opinion on something, Chief Justice."

I rose. So did Jonata.

"Given the circumstances, none of the clergy will leave without an escort," my warden said firmly.

The second officer shrugged. "Take it up with the captain."

Jonata and I followed Little Squirrel up to the quarterdeck.

My warden murmured, "Overcast sky with the storm clouds much closer."

If Titus was taking us closer to the storm his first officer warned us about, things weren't going in our favor. Sea Wolf was still at the wheel as we approached the captain.

Without a preamble, Titus held out his distance-viewer to me. "Something's wrong with the five ships pursuing us. We need your sight, Chief Justice."

"Five?" One of Luc's curses in the Cantan language sprang to mind, but I didn't say the obscene words aloud.

Titus nodded. "Off the port side."

I braced myself against the railing and peered through the distance-viewer in the direction the captain indicated. What Little Squirrel had referred to as langskips were much closer now. They were long, narrow wooden vessels with what appeared to be a single deck. A single mast rose from the center of the ships, but the only langskip with a sail rigged was the one almost directly behind us, using the trade winds like the *Mars Tranquilus*. Poles extended from the sides. No, not poles. Oars.

But it was the things rowing the langskips that sent a shiver through me.

I lowered the distance-viewer and turned to Titus. "Let me guess. A langskip on oars only shouldn't be able to match speeds with a caravel under full sail."

He shook his head.

I swallowed the bile at the back of my throat. "The reason they are gaining on us is because they are crewed by skinwalkers."

Chapter 17

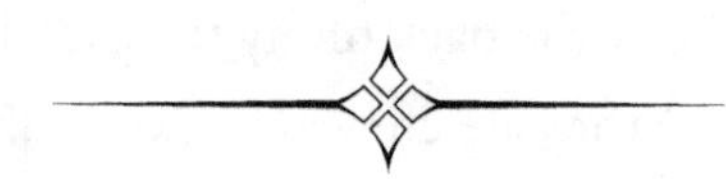

I waited for Titus's reaction.

He pursed his lips and stared at our pursuers for a long moment. "One demon nearly killed everyone in the Jing Embassy. And after what happened to Tandor—" He shook his head at his memories of his two encounters with the alien invaders.

"The odds are they're carrying demon eggs," I said. "Any survivors will be used to hatch them. And Twelve help us if they are carrying even one full grown demon with them. But the skinwalkers are humans with talent practicing demon magic. We are terribly outnumbered with them alone."

Titus nodded sharply as if his decision was made. "Ninety degrees to starboard! Strike the sails! Break out the sea fire!" His orders echoed through the ship.

He turned back to me and Jonata. "Any spells in your arsenal that can keep those skinwalkers busy would be a huge assistance to the ship's defense, Chief Justice."

I grinned. "We'll see what we can do, Captain."

Jonata and I returned to the captain's cabin and quickly explained the situation. I finished with my proposal. "Yin Li, Shi Hua, and I will keep the skinwalkers occupied with spells while the crew keeps us afloat."

"I can—" Luc started.

"High Brother, we are sailing into a Peaceful Sea winter storm while being chased by skinwalkers." I gestured to indicate myself and the other two priestesses. "The three of us will have to wear ropes to keep from being swept overboard. I need one Light person to keep an eye on the crown prince, and right now, you're the only one from Light who doesn't want to toss Quan overboard."

"Are you sure about that?" Luc said dryly.

"Would you prefer we rig the catapult and toss you at the skinwalkers chasing us?" I shot back.

"You know she will do it, High Brother," Yar said. "Please do not make Mateqai and me explain your death to Chief Warden Nicholas."

"Personally, I would prefer not to be lashed for other peoples' idiocy," Mateqai growled.

Luc glared at his wardens before he held up his hands in surrender. "Fine. I'll assist Yin Shang in protecting the crown prince."

It amazed me how much resentment he could pack into that singular statement while pleasing a young child by taking the boy seriously.

The other two priestesses followed me to the other cabin where we quickly changed clothing. For Shi Hua and me, our Temple robes would become sodden with rain and sea water, making it difficult to fight effectively. Yin Li ditched her proper Jing ladies' wear as well for clothing similar to the crew of the *Mars Tranquilus*.

We all grabbed a handhold when the ship shuddered as if something slammed into us. Shi Hua cocked her head. "A wave hit us broadside."

She donned a similar wool jacket and pants to the ones I pulled out of my trunk. Bless Sivan for thinking ahead. And we all went barefoot like the crew, too. Last thing we needed was for our standard Temple boots or Yin Li's silk ladies slippers to slide us right into the icy arms of the Peaceful Sea.

We exited the cabin in time to see a wave taller than the ship's main mast. Out of instinct, I raised my hands and froze the time around the gigantic swell. The *Mars Tranquilus* swept past it out of sheer momentum. I released the wave.

Behind us, wood splintered with a horrendous boom, which was quickly followed by screams louder than the howling wind. A cheer swept through the crew.

"Ladies!" Titus bellowed. "Get up to the aftcastle! Pilot, turn us into the wind!"

Salt spray burned our eyes as the Jing priestesses and I scrambled up past the quarterdeck to the aftcastle. Bits and pieces of one of the langskips danced on the surface behind us. Gray-green heads bobbed here and there, but the sea herself seemed determined to swallow them as the perversions they were.

Little Squirrel and another male sailor helped us don harnesses with lines anchored to the ships railings. The smaller woman grinned, the same wild one High Brother Jax wore in the middle of a battle.

"Excellent blow, m'lady!" Little Squirrel slapped my back.

Both Yin Li and Shi Hua carried their bows and full quivers of arrows. I recognized the sealed jars in boxes tied to the deck. Twelve bless Titus, he'd anticipated an attack despite our efforts to keep our journey fast and quiet. The first langskip I had spotted was gaining on us after Titus's maneuvers to get us into the edge of the storm.

"Little Squirrel! Aim the catapult at that ship!" I pointed at the langskip in question.

"Our catapult doesn't have that kind of range!"

"It doesn't need to!" I knew my grin was as wild as hers. She nodded and issued orders. Yin Li, Shi Hua, and I helped the crew adjust the catapult's aim. The arm was winched down by two of the sailors. The other two carefully loaded the sealed jar.

Or as carefully as they could with the way the *Mars Tranquilus* was being tossed about by the waves. Breaking a jar of sea fire on board our ship would result in our own destruction. Splatters of pale green rain finished wetting down any surface that had escaped the blue-ish green spray.

"On your command!" she shouted at me.

"Shi Hua?"

The Jing Light priestess already had an arrow nocked. "Charged or uncharged?"

"Uncharged," I shouted back. "No sense wasting your magic just yet." I counted the dips and rises as the langskip pursued us.

"Fire one!"

The crew released the rope. The arm swung upward. The jar sailed through the air. At the height of its arc, I froze the bubble of time around it.

The skinwalkers jeered and taunted us until they realized the jar wasn't going to splash harmlessly into the water.

"Fire two!"

Shi Hua released her arrow. Her aim, as always, was true. I freed time around the jar filled with sea fire as a swell raised the langskip's bow nearly to the jar's height. Shi Hua's arrow cracked open the jar. Rain and sea spray did the rest.

The entire front half of the langskip was engulfed in flames before their captain could order the rowers to reverse course. More screams of pain and fear battled the wind for the loudest sound. With the slightest push of time forward to speed along the flames, the entire ship was on fire as it started to sink.

The odd thing about sea fire was one or two of the minerals in it burned when they touched water. The langskip was still burning when the waves swallowed it, and the pinkish glow confirmed the ship continued to burn as it descended the depths.

That left three more enemy vessels.

Rain turned from pale green drops to sheets of solid purple. Despite

Sea Wolf fighting the wheel to keep us on course, the storm pulled us further into itself.

However, our pursuers were not discouraged one bit by either the weather or the fates of their compatriots. Four skinwalkers stood next to the langskip's mast, probably tied in place like we were. The sour prickle of demon magic raised the fine hairs along my skin.

"Wards!" I yelled, raising my own as I shouted the order.

Light energy flared to my left, and Shi Hua stumbled back from the force of the demon magic thrown at her. I extended my own wards barely in time to bounce the second spell back at the closest ship.

Damn, the skinwalkers! I should have left Shi Hua in the cabin with Luc. Of course, our enemies would target her first.

Pink-white light flashed as the deflected skinwalker spell hit the water. I winced and ducked my head at the painful brightness.

"Anthea!" Shi Hua shrieked. "What's wrong?"

"The water!" Panic filled Little Squirrel's voice. "What in Wildling is that thing?"

I wiped the tears, rain, and sea water from my face. I caught sight of what frightened the sailor, and my heart threatened to erupt from my chest and throw itself overboard.

The water boiled around what appeared to be a hole in time and space. The black tentacles emerging from the portal filled my throat with gorge. Their color was the same as a demon's.

Balance help us, that had been a summoning spell!

And whatever was emerging into our world was no simple demon. The spell itself would have torn the *Mars Tranquilus* apart. And if by some miracle the ship remained afloat, the tentacle creature would finished the job.

"Little Squirrel, target that creature!" I bellowed. My order shook the four sailors out of their shock. They scrambled to shift the catapult.

The skinwalkers probably sensed Luc in the cabin below us because they focused their magic on our end of the ship. Somehow, Yin Li managed to shield all of us on the aftcastle from additional demon magic spells.

"Shi Hua, keep those damn skinwalkers distracted!"

She braced herself and started launching charged arrows at the langskip attempting to close in on the *Mars Tranquilus* while Yin Li continued to ward us from the skinwalkers' spells. The storm made it difficult for both ships to gain any advantage, not with the creature's waving tentacles nearby.

Shi Hua's arrows were nothing more than pin pricks to the beast attempting to birth itself into our world. The priestess would occasionally strike one of the rowers on the langskip, but the quartet casting spells were warding their people just as we were. I assisted the sailors in adjusting the catapult.

"Launch four of the sea fire jars as fast as you can," I said to Little Squirrel. "Don't worry about accuracy."

She nodded, and they set to work. Now that our ship had turned into the wind, we started to slow our forward motion. The rowers of the langskip used their superior strength to circle around the rip in dimensions and the creature. I pushed away my terror that we were severely outmatched, and I tried to visualize what my birth father Kilchii would do. He never showed his fear when Tandor was under siege. Those memories comforted me despite a flailing tentacle throwing a huge amount of sea water across the aftcastle.

I swiped the salt water from my face and braced myself. The crewmembers launched the first jar. I slowed the time around the ceramic. The same maneuvers let all four jars to float over the rip between dimensions.

An arrow from Shi Hua struck one of the standing skinwalkers, and he slumped. The closest rower cut the sorcerer's line, and his body tumbled into the wildly bubbling sea. The rift flickered for a moment. His companions were holding the portal open. We needed to kill them, or at least break their concentration.

I sped up the last three jars. They smashed into the first jar, and I released the time bubble. The rain ignited the sea fire as it fell into the creature.

It emitted the most horrendous howl. Tentacles thrashed, and one slammed into the langskip midship. Wood snapped and cracked as the langskip split in two. Bodies were flung through the air. The portal flashed shut, leaving severed tentacles in its wake. Instead of the pop of displaced air, both sea and air roared into the void.

And the water dragged the *Mars Tranquilus* into the rapidly filling cavity where the enormous dimensional rip had been a moment before.

Chapter 18

I desperately held onto the railing as did the others on the aftcastle. The water's movement reminded me too much of Brother Sisquoc of Wildling caught in the flash flood last fall on our way to Diné. I couldn't freeze the Peaceful Sea. There was nothing by which to anchor the spell.

After all my shouting since the skinwalker ships intercepted us, my throat was raw. I reached out and touched Titus's mind. *Captain?*

I could feel him physically jerk. *Chief Justice?*

Turn into the spin of the water, I said.

The vortex will pull my ship apart, he argued.

Not if we're moving fast enough, I said. *I can speed up time and use the vortex to throw us free.*

"Brace yourselves!" he bellowed. "Wheel hard to port!"

Despite my toes and heels wedged against the railing, I started to slide thanks to the ship's tilt at an alarming angle. One of the sailors manning the catapult snagged the collar of my wool coat and hauled me upright. He used his body to keep me in place.

I took the opportunity to concentrate on the words and gestures of the spell I needed. The *Mars Tranquilus* spun around the edge of the vortex.

Now, I whispered in Titus's mind at the same time he shouted the order to straighten the rudder. The ship shot out of the vortex, heading in the opposite direction of the two surviving langskips.

"Forgive my impertinence, m'lady," the sailor who had kept me from dangling over the vortex said.

"Saving my hide wasn't impertinent." I smiled at him. "Thank you."

We were now in the full rage of the storm. Lightning flashed overhead, followed instantly by a deafening *boom*.

"Best you and the sisters get down to the cabin, m'lady." The sailor unhooked my harness. "It's going to be a rough night."

After Shi Hua, Yin Li, and I changed into dry clothing, all of the passengers huddled in the captain's cabin through the rest of the night. No one could get any sleep between the howl of the wind and pitch and roll of the rough seas.

Sivan, Istaqa, and the Jing embassy's head of household had packed plenty of Master Healer Bly's potion for upset stomachs. We were all nauseated by the tossing of the *Mars Tranquilus*. However, Huizhong, one of Quan's guards, was allergic to peppermint, and he couldn't take the stomach remedy. The poor man spent a good portion of the night vomiting into a chamber pot until I insisted he take two drops of soma tears.

He tried to present a stoic façade, but it was hard to maintain a brave demeanor with his face in a bronze waste container. Finally, Quan threatened to unman Huizhong with his own entrails if he didn't take the soma tears. Once Huizhong started snoring, everyone relaxed a hair.

I leaned my head against Luc's shoulder. The creaks and groans of the wood made the ship sound like a living creature in pain.

"What do you think the skinwalkers in the other two ships will do?" he murmured.

"Row clear of the storm," I said. "Use the trade winds to get ahead of the *Mars Tranquilus* again. That's what I'd do if our positions were reversed."

Yin Shang had snuggled between me and his mother with his own blanket. He peered up at me though I was sure he couldn't see me in the dark. "Chief Justice, may I ask you a question?"

"Of course," I said.

"Why is it we never pray to Balance for help?"

Both Luc and I chuckled.

"That is a question even Her own order has been debating since Child first created humans," I said.

"But Mother says you help people," the boy continued. "It doesn't make sense Balance would ignore our prayers if her own priestesses help people."

"Balance knows the wisdom of when to interfere and when not to," I said. "Your mother did not carry you in her arms forever. If she tried, your legs might become stunted, and you would never learn to walk on your own. But if you injured your leg, she would carry you again until you could walk again."

"Or like how the healers and the smiths worked together to create High Brother Luc's special crutches?" Yin Shang blurted with enthusiasm.

Yin Li made a disapproving sound low in her throat.

Give your son's curiosity free rein, Sister, I said silently. *It's keeping both him and the others distracted from the storm.*

If you say so, Chief Justice. But her mental voice didn't sound happy. I wondered how much of her bad tamper was exhaustion and how much was her annoyance of having to spend the night in the same cabin as Quan after she'd made a scene earlier.

As if in answer to my comment on ignoring the storm, the *Mars Tranquilus* dove into a trough. We all slammed into the person next to us with poor Luc at the bottom of the pile against the bulkhead. He let out a muffled grunt.

When the ship righted itself, Luc said, "Unfortunately, our genius healers and smiths cannot invent crutches that prevent me from getting crushed by my fellow passengers."

Yin Shang giggled.

"Son, why don't you sit on my lap?" Yin Li patted her thighs.

"A warrior doesn't sit on his mother's lap." The boy's lower lip jutted out in defiance. Even though Yin Li couldn't see his expression in their dark, the tone of his voice was sufficient to raise her ire.

"A Temple warrior doesn't argue with his superior even if she is his mother," Yar chided gently. "I must obey Sister Yin Li because she outranks me. Just as you would have to obey me as a warden because you are not yet a novice. And right now, as your superior, she is looking out for your safety as any great leader would do."

"Yes, Warden Yar," Yin Shang said contritely. "Mother, I am sorry for offering you insult."

"Your apology is accepted, my son." Yin Li's tone was a mix of exasperation, worry, and affection.

Maybe it was a good thing I could not bear children after all. I doubt if I could maintain the level of patience both Yar and Yin Li exhibited.

Once Yin Shang was settled on his mother's lap, he continued to ask me questions about a number of subjects from novice life to Diné culture. The roar of the wind died to a mere grumbling before the boy fell asleep from sheer exhaustion.

Chapter 19

Oddly, it was the silence that jerked me awake. No laughter or shouting of orders outside the cabin door. I leaned against the crook of Luc's left shoulder with his arm around my body. Yin Shang's legs were draped over mine. Everyone about me was sound asleep.

Everyone except Quan who wasn't in the cabin at all.

Panic seized me, and I carefully extricated myself and my robes from the limbs around me. I tried to walk silently to the cabin door, but one of Jonata's eyes opened from where she was curled on a hammock with Long Feather.

I shook my head and held my finger to my lips. She nodded and closed her eye again. Quan must have used his limited Thief talent to creep out of the cabin without his guards or our wardens hearing him.

Warmth struck my face. The bloody globe of the sun had risen two handspans above the horizon, and the trade winds caught my hood and pushed it back from my face. The ship was aimed in the wrong direction.

First Officer Iniki directed roughly half the crew in repairs, including the Jing crown prince. When I approached Iniki, he bobbed his head.

"Good morntide, Chief Justice."

"I trust we made it through the night without any losses, First Officer," I replied.

He chuckled. "The only losses were our pride and torn sail thanks to debris from one of the langskips."

I shook my head. "I'd say the Twelve blessed us, considering we were outnumbered and our opposition were skinwalkers."

Iniki nodded. "Exactly what the captain said, m'lady." He hesitated a moment before he added, "I know at the time we didn't show appropriate courtesy to you, but thank you for investigating Captain Arturo's death properly and clearing the crew's names."

It wasn't too often someone bothered to apologize to me when it came to a case in my jurisdiction. I nodded. "You're welcome, First Officer." A wry smile tightened my face. "Is there anything we can do to help in the repairs besides offering Prince Po's services?"

Iniki grinned. "He knows our business surprisingly well, but if you're volunteering and not trying to be polite . . ."

Within a candlemark, everyone, both crew and passengers, on the *Mars Tranquilus* was awake and put to work. Not even Yin Shang complained when he was told to assist his mother and Luc in preparing a hot meal for everyone. Apparently, Yar's admonishment last night had made an impression on the boy.

It wasn't long before the line and sails had been repaired. Shortly past Second Afternoon according to the position of the sun, Captain Titus ordered the partial raising of the sails. Sea Wolf steered the ship into a careful one-hundred eighty degree turn. With the sails fully raised and catching the trade winds, a cheer went up from everyone because we were underway again.

However, Titus called a quick conference with his officers, the prince, and the clergy. The lines on his brow definitely weren't from the weather.

"This is the fragment from the last langskip destroyed." Titus held up a piece of wood. "The debris that ripped through one of our sails. It's teak, not oak."

"For those of us who aren't sailors, the significance is what?" Yin Li asked.

"Teak is used for shipbuilding in the southeastern parts of the Old Continent," Quan said. "Whereas the langskip design was used in the northwestern section of the Old Continent, and the Skandza use oak."

"Could teak saplings been imported and planted on a nearby island?" I asked.

"There are very few islands in this area that have sufficient fresh water to grow trees, much less cultivate trees large enough with which to build the langskips," Little Squirrel commented.

"Where could these skinwalkers have reinforcements?" Titus asked while pointedly looking at me.

"I'm not even sure where the five ships could have come from." I waved my hand to indicate southeast from the *Mars Tranquilus*. "We're hundreds of leagues from O'ahu. And they are the northernmost of the Sea Peoples territories."

"No offense, m'lady, but O'ahu is that way," Iniki pointed to the northeast. "We sailed south to hit the Equatorial Current in order to make better time."

"If we're that far south, shouldn't we be seeing Sea Peoples' vessels?" Shi Hua asked.

"Yes." The lines on Titus's forehead grew deeper.

"But not every island between here and the Kingdom of Ryukyu is inhabited, is it?" I asked.

"No," Iniki said. "Many of them are far too low to build on, most don't have a source of fresh water, and they flood with sea water during storms."

I turned to Luc. "Do you remember ever seeing the skinwalkers in Tandor ever eating or drinking?"

He shook his head. "That would explain part of the skinwalker transformation process. They are probably being sustained by the demon magic they're using. Somehow."

"So they wouldn't need to eat or drink," Shi Hua finished.

"The flaw with that idea is demons do need to eat," I said.

"What if it's a side effect of using demon magic?" Quan said. "At least for humans. We need to drink water, but demons don't."

Titus cleared his throat. "While the scholarly debate on demon habits is intriguing, it does not help in our mission to reach Jing intact."

Luc eyed me. "You need to tell him your theory. You understand the demons better than anyone else living who is not a renegade."

I hugged myself against the wave of cold that had burrowed into my bones. It seemed to be a side effect from when the dead demons forming a grimoire tried to seduce me into joining them. It hadn't gone away despite the Temple of Child clearing me to return to my duties. "We know two of the langskips survived and retreated. If our positions were reversed, I would have withdrawn from the storm, caught the trade winds, and attempt to intercept my foes again."

Titus exhaled gustily. "Then we will see them again since we are still a fortnight from Ryukyu. Thank you for your honesty, Chief Justice."

"They aren't going to use the same tactics as they did before," Luc warned.

Iniki laughed. "Unless they wait until the next storm in seven days."

"I'm more worried there are additional ships out there," I muttered.

"I thought my safety was more important," Quan quipped.

"The option to throw you overboard is still open." I smiled sweetly. "I suggest you speak with your advisor before both of your bodyguards stab you and use you as fish bait."

Chapter 20

Later that night, Luc and I found ourselves in the empty storeroom once again. This time though, it was damp and uncomfortable despite Luc's warming spell.

"Rain and sea water everywhere." I spread out my robes for us to sit on. "It almost makes me miss the arid winds and oil scraping of Diné."

"I expected you to complain about the lack of bathing long before now." Luc chuckled as he lowered himself to my robes. "Even when we were on circuit, as long as you could bathe, even in the iciest streams, you were happy."

"True," I admitted before I made a show of sniffing my arm pit. "I can barely stand the smell of myself. I don't know how anyone else can tolerate it."

"I like the way you smell," he said softly.

Warm tingles that had nothing to do with his magic danced along my skin. I raised an eyebrow. "Truly? You're trying to seduce me? Here? Now?"

"The key word here is trying," he said a little crossly. "Last night was the closest I've been to losing you."

"We all would have died if not for Titus and his crew's skill—" I started.

"I meant the battle with the skinwalkers." He looked away for a long moment before he added, "I always knew deep in my spirit you would defeat Gerd, and we worked together in Tandor, but this . . ."

I sat beside him, took his left hand in my right, and leaned my head against his shoulder. "I couldn't even think of failing during our encounter with the langskips. Not with you on board the ship. I know Quan is supposed to be our priority, but he wasn't yesterday." I lifted Luc's hand and kissed it.

"Light help us, we will live through this voyage and get Quan his damn throne," he said fiercely. "And we will make a point of stopping at the Kingdom of O'ahu for a few days on the way home. I hear it's a beautiful place."

"That sounds lovely," I said. "We can enjoy the sun, try some of the dishes Lailani has mentioned, and maybe see a whale pod as they head north."

"I think we could both use a little peace and quiet," he murmured against my hair. "Like now."

I looked up at him, and I decided a little bit of pleasure now wouldn't hurt anyone. I warded the room and let Luc kiss me senseless.

Unfortunately, our interlude was briefer than either of us would have liked. We had a marital contract to finish negotiating.

I glanced at the notes I'd stamped while discussing matters with Shi Hua after the *Mars Tranquilus* had resumed her original course. "The sister is willing to forgo the estate and yearly allowance for her parents on the condition that the prince no longer keeps any secrets from her."

Luc blinked. "That was going to be part of his counter. His alternate suggestion was in lieu of the estate and allowance, her parents will be given a suite in the imperial palace. He would prefer their children have some family close by."

I stared at Luc. "Quan really said that?"

Luc shrugged. "Despite the political pig manure between their fathers, he and his brother were quite close. The emperor's death hit Quan far harder than he wishes to acknowledge."

I swallowed hard. "He admitted to me when we first left Orrin the empress was expecting their third child."

"Oh." Luc exhaled heavily. "I guess I should have known."

"Known what?"

A wry smile tilted the corner of his mouth. "Why he choose me to negotiate on his behalf."

I tried to follow Luc's logic, but I finally had to admit, "I don't understand."

"He knew you would do your damnedest to make sure Shi Hua and her family were taken care of, and he knew I'd call him on his attitude without stabbing him."

I grinned. "But stabbing him would be so much fun."

"I believe he would prefer a different type of stabbing with you," Luc said dryly.

I groaned. "Are we back to that?"

Luc stared at me. "I don't think he was making a jest when he suggested you become his wife and Shi Hua your surrogate."

I shook my head. "Whatever his true feelings for me, he knows he cannot marry me. It would be a very idiotic political move, and Quan is not an idiot though sometimes, he plays at being one. I'm barren, Luc. I cannot give him a child any more than I can give you one. And he needs an heir. He needs one desperately. He is too aware he is the last Bao. The last thing he wants is the damn throne and to force Shi Hua into a loveless marriage, but the alternative is to watch the Jing Empire collapse. And maybe all of humanity with it."

Luc reached for my hand, and I placed my palm in his.

I'm sorry, my love. I let my own emotions get in the way.

You mean your illegal ones? I teased.

You don't have to be so literal about it, he grumbled.

I'm not the one letting a foreign prince get under my skin, I said. *And he only makes advances at me because he enjoys irritating you.*

"Shall we deliver the news to our principals?" Luc said out loud.

I groaned again. "Do we have to do it right at this moment?"

"The sooner we do, the sooner everyone is back in their own beds," he said.

"Point taken." I stood and helped him to his foot. "Let's get this contract finalized."

Chapter 21

Quan, Shi Hua, Luc and I sat at the table in the captain's cabin as we reviewed what we hoped would be the final form of their marital contract.

"You two realize this is all dependent on whether the Reverend Father of Light grants your petition, don't you?" I said.

"We've already submitted our petition," Shi Hua said.

"When?" I said incredulously.

"We've been in discussions with him for the last two weeks," Quan said.

"And he said if we could come to an acceptable agreement between the two of us, he would grant my dispensation to leave the order," Shi Hua added.

"I'm impressed your Reverend Father was that amenable to the idea," Luc commented.

"He understands the political situation with the nobles." From the way Shi Hua tightly gripped her tea cup, it was a wonder the fine ceramic didn't shatter. "My Light abilities outweigh my origins."

"What's that supposed to mean?" I growled.

"Nothing, m'lady," she murmured, but she wouldn't meet my gaze.

"Shi Hua, I cannot do my duty as your representative if you haven't told me everything."

"I am of common birth," she whispered.

"And?" I prompted.

Her head jerked up, and her anger poked hotly against my psyche. "I worry the nobility will use that fact against my future husband."

I frowned and glared at Quan. "You haven't told her about your father?"

"I did," the crown prince said dryly. "That's part of her worry."

I turned back to Shi Hua. "I apologize, Sister, but this must be a Jing cultural aspect I do not understand. Please explain it to me as you would your cousin Yin Shang."

Her throat bobbed. "Po has only his mother's blood to connect him to the throne."

"And that is not sufficient?" I asked.

She sighed before she poured herself some more tea. "The Chumash didn't have a noble class prior to the Battle of Apache Tears and the formation of Issura."

I smiled. "I'm aware of our queendom's history."

"It's why your people don't take the noble class as seriously as you take the Temples or Guilds. Those positions are generally earned, not bestowed." She took a sip of her tea. "However, the noble class in Jing has existed since long before Balance's warning about the demons. They do hold a great deal of power and influence, and they can make or break whoever sits on the Dragon Throne."

"As shown by their refusal to accept my father as the imperial consort," Quan added.

"But surely, Reverend Father Biming and the rest of Thief have started a whisper campaign in your favor, haven't they?" Luc said.

"There's a campaign of similar strength from those who resent Emperor Bao Chengwu's execution of the members of the School of Sorcery." Shi Hua shook her head. "I don't think either the emperor or the Temples realized how deep the school had their talons in the nobility until now."

"What exactly are we up against?" I asked.

"A distant cousin of mine, Zixin, claims he has a superior right to the throne because he has a mix of imperial and noble blood," Quan said sourly.

"And from your expression, he's more interest in the power than protecting his people from demons," Luc said.

Quan smiled. "Unfortunate, but true. Otherwise, I'd relinquish my claim to the throne in a heartbeat."

I leaned back and stared at the ceiling. Apparently, the Temples in Issura weren't the only ones that had been infiltrated. Word had gotten out that Quan was already on his way home. It explained the skinwalkers sent to intercept the *Mars Tranquilus*.

"We really should have brought a weather wizard with us," I muttered. "Or taken out the other two langskips."

"Thief blessed us with the luck and skills to destroy three and escape relatively unscathed," Luc said.

I lifted my head and looked at him. "And the odds are one of the other two had a distance speaker with them, which is why they held back from engaging us."

"Surely, the storm—" Quan began.

"The other three didn't hesitate one bit in the face of the weather or the maelstrom they created when their spell to tear an opening into the demon dimension landed in the sea." I shook my head. "They'll contact this Zixin, and—"

"Slow down," Luc said with a scowl. "You can't dance into Chengzhou and randomly accuse someone of consorting with demons."

"The demons and skinwalkers play on our deepest desires." Weariness dragged on my flesh. Part of me hated that I knew how the blasted things thought and worked. "If Zixin honestly thinks he's better suited to rule Jing than Quan, no matter how misguided his feelings, the renegades and their allies will use that to their advantage and corrupt him."

Shi Hua looked at Quan. "Would Zixin know about the secret passage into the imperial palace?"

"In theory, no." He shrugged. "But that doesn't mean the information wasn't passed down through his branch of the family. He traces his ancestry to Empress Bao De's youngest daughter, whereas mine runs through the empress's eldest child. Each of our grandparents would have known about the passage."

I rubbed my temples. Another ache had settled behind my eyes. "Does Reverend Father Biming know about this cousin of yours?"

"Yes, and before you ask, he does have eyes on Zixin," Quan said.

"Yes, well, Reverend Father Gray Shadow thought he had ears on Reverend Mother Alara, too." I couldn't help the sarcasm in my voice. The situation with Justice Melanippe bothered me more than I cared to admit. Even with friends looking out for her, she disappeared without a trace.

Had I done the wrong thing by coming to Jing? Had I put Yanaba and her son in danger by leaving them alone? Elizabeth and Erato would be leaving Orrin soon for their assignments.

"All we can do is prepare for the inevitable attack before we reach Jing," Luc said.

"Does this mean the contract is ready for signing?" Quan asked.

"Not yet, Po." Shi Hua laid her hand on his. "I cannot sign it prior to being released from my vows. We cannot take the chance this contract or our marriage is overturned on a legal technicality." She turned to me. "We need to wait until we hear from Reverend Father Jin."

"That's more than acceptable to us," Luc said.

"We need to take all our scribbles and combine them into one document anyway," I said. "You're going to want to have multiple copies." I shook my head. "If I'd known I was going to have to do this much legal work on our journey, I would have brought Donella with me."

"You mean dragged Donella along with you," Luc teased.

"I think we'd better adjourn before our representatives come to blows," Shi Hua said with a smirk.

"Or kisses," Quan said.

I groaned. "Have we reached Jing yet?"

Chapter 22

During our next contact with Reverend Father Biming later that night, Reverend Father Jin of Light participated and assured Shi Hua he had signed her grant of disposition to wed Crown Prince Po. The only kink was when Reverend Father Jin asked me to officiate Shi Hua and Po's wedding on board the *Mars Tranquilus*.

I understand the necessity to finalize the matter as soon as possible, I said. *But why not have the wedding when we reach Chengzhou?*

Not to be indelicate, Reverend Father Biming said. *If the ceremony is already done, the prince and his wife can consummate their relationship.*

You want Shi Hua's womb seeded before we arrive? I couldn't keep the disbelief from my mental voice. *She already had one difficult birth two months ago, and we don't have a healer on board! I won't allow you to use her in that manner!*

Reverend Father Biming laughed while a wave of embarrassment flowed from Reverend Father Jin. On the other hand, Shi Hua kept a tight lid on her emotions.

Surprisingly, none of them argued an Issuran justice had no jurisdiction over a Jing civilian. I hoped Justice Mei Wen recovered enough to aid Shi Hua in legal matters. The future empress was going to need all the friends she had to survive.

Was this your idea, Reverend Father Jin? I ranted. *I thought Issura's Reverend Father of Light was a sick, perverted piece of work.*

I meant no harm to Sister, rather, Mistress Shi Hua, he blurted. *I'm afraid my knowledge of certain . . . things are lacking.*

I forced myself to take a deep breath before I said something I would truly regret. Queen Teodora expected me to aid Crown Prince Po, but Balance help me, I wasn't going to let him or any other man in Jing to ill-use the young woman.

The prince may consummate the marriage as a formality, but Mistress Shi Hua needs another ten months before she should even try to conceive again. I paused for emphasis. *I will put that in the marital contract. If I find out any of you have violated her trust, I will return to Chengzhou and unman every single idiot involved.*

The chief justice is not jesting, Reverend Fathers, Quan said. *And I, for one, do not wish to find myself on the sharp end of her blades.*

Shouldn't Sister Yin Li perform the ceremony as our only Jing Temple representative present? Luc asked.

There are already those who would question Shi Hua's intentions toward Prince Po, Reverend Father Biming said. *If her maternal aunt performs the ceremony, we would add ammunition to those who are spreading nasty rumors about him.*

You mean Zixin, I said sourly. *Does he even have a talent?*

None that we know of, Reverend Father Jin said. *His stance is the Temples manipulated the emperor into executing the members of the School of Sorcery.*

That rather tilts my opinion of who was behind the attack on the Mars Tranquilus, I snapped.

Or the renegades could be using him, Luc pointed out.

Either way, if we could catch Zixin meeting with a renegade or another sympathizer, we would have someone to question, Reverend Father Biming said.

I am more worried about the spy within your ranks who found out Quan was already on his way home, I said.

As are we, Chief Justice, Reverend Father Jin snapped. *Your Temples in Issura aren't the only ones being targeted.*

Let us calm down, Reverend Father Biming said. *We don't need to do the work of the renegades for them.*

Luc rested his hand on my shoulder. His warmth and affection flooded me, but it didn't lessen my irritation with the Jing clergy.

Then we're going to need to extend our stop in Ryukyu, I said. *We can alter some of Yin Li's civilian clothing, but Shi Hua is going to need a trousseau befitting the wife of a crown prince and future empress.*

Thank you for your assistance, Chief Justice, Reverend Father Biming said. *Please keep the receipts so we can reimburse you.*

When we ended contact with those in Jing, I opened my eyes to find Quan scowling at me.

"Do you think I cannot take care of my future wife?" he growled.

"In Issura, the woman's family provides her new clothing to start her married life." I shrugged. "Shi Hua only has Yin Li and me, and we will make sure she's ready to make an impression when we reach Jing."

When we retired for the night, everyone was back in their original cabins. Both Shi Hua and Yin Li had forgiven Quan once he made appropriate apologies to both women.

Even though Luc, our four wardens, and I had settled in our respective bed or hammocks, the wardens expressed their concerns about the situation we were sailing into. Well, three of them did. Mateqai remained strangely silent.

Should I address his silence? Luc asked me silently. I buried my face in his shoulder to keep from laughing out loud at his unintentional joke.

Yes. I giggled. *You need to deal with the possibility of his transfer.*

Luc cleared his throat. "Mateqai?"

"Yes, High Brother?"

"You haven't said anything about potential problems over the next two weeks," Luc prodded.

"My colleagues covered everything I would have addressed," Mateqai said.

"Is there anything else we need to discuss?" Luc continued.

It was a good thing none of my cabin mates could see the faces I made. This dancing around the subject was worse than negotiating the stupid marital contract.

"I do not believe so, High Brother," Mateqai answered.

Jonata rose up on her elbows, which sent her and Long Feather's hammock swaying. "Oh, for the love of Balance, the high brother wants to know if you're planning to resign from the Temples and stay in Jing under Mistress Shi Hua's employ."

Everyone looked in Mateqai's direction even though he was just a shadow to them.

"She has not asked me to do so," the warden said stiffly.

"Because she doesn't want to ask you to make the decision between her and the high brother," I said softly. "This is a question of what do you want."

"Over the last year and a half, so many things have changed," Mateqai murmured. "I'm not sure what I want."

"Chief Warden Catherine is still writing to you, isn't she?" Yar rumbled.

"Yes," Mateqai replied.

"Who's Chief Warden Catherine?" I asked. She wasn't any of Orrin's Temple guards.

"She serves High Sister Imala of Love in Standora," Mateqai said. "We were classmates at the Wardens Academy, and we renewed our acquaintance when we marched south to Tandor last spring."

"And Shi Hua knows you've been in contact with Catherine?" I asked.

"Yes, m'lady." Mateqai exhaled. "Chief Warden Catherine has asked me to transfer to Love. However, Mistress Shi Hua is going into a dangerous situation with no one to guard her back. And my loyalty should be to the high brother, not to either woman."

"Mateqai, there is no perfect solution to your situation," Luc said. "However, if you wish to transfer to the Standoran Temple of Love or stay in Jing as the future empress's bodyguard, you have my blessing."

"And if it's any consolation, you're not the only one who's worried about Shi Hua," I added.

"Thank you for your counsel, High Brother, Chief Justice." Mateqai released a deep breath before he added, "I will consider your words and give you an answer before we reach Jing."

I didn't envy the warden's position any more than I envied Quan and Shi Hua's. Part of me wanted to find one of those uninhabited islands and bury my head in the sand.

Chapter 23

The next morning, all of the female passengers gathered in my cab-in, and we took stock of what we had to work with to provide Shi Hua a trousseau befitting her new social status. I placed my bag of gold on the table. Jonata laughed as Yin Li peered inside.

The Love priestess looked at me in amazement. "You're Temple! How did you get this much money?"

Shi Hua shook her head. "I'm not taking your Mill winnings, Anthea."

"It's not all of my winnings," I retorted. "And I was serious about out-fitting you properly. You need to look like a noblewoman." I smiled. "A well-armed noblewoman though your weapons should not be visible."

"I already feel odd not wearing my Temple uniform," she murmured. Jonata had loaned Shi Hua a civilian skirt and tunic. Unfortunately, her feet were even tinier than Jonata's, so she was forced to wear her uniform boots.

"We need a list of what to wear." I dug a bottle of ink, a small pa-pyrus roll, a bag of sand, and a quill from my case and passed them to Jonata. "Shoes need to be at the top of the list."

I turned to Shi Hua. "What is the official mourning period when the Jing ruler dies?"

"A year," she said softly. "I will need one or two outfits in white. That's our color of mourning."

Jonata looked up from the papyrus at the former priestess's peculiar tone. "Shi Hua, if you've changed your mind about leaving the Temple of Light, you know you can go back. It's not too late."

A wan smile crossed the other woman's face. "I haven't changed my mind. I—" She swiped at the tear that escaped with the back of her hand. "This morning, I told Jeremy about me wedding Po."

"Oh," I breathed. "How did he take the news?"

"He asked me why." She sniffed. "W-why I choose to marry Quan wh-when—"

Yin Li pulled her niece into her arms. "You didn't do anything wrong. You did your duty to the Temples, and now, you're doing your duty to your emperor and your nation."

"I never wanted to hurt him," Shi Hua wailed. "I told him at the beginning I couldn't love him, not romantically anyway. Now, when he looks at Chao—"

"Stop right there," I said as gently as I could. "First of all, give Jeremy some credit. He would never hurt Chao. Twelve forbid he even thinks about it, Mya will talk him through his feelings. Not to mention, the chief wardens will never let anyone touch the Light children. They've had a plan for some time to get you mothers and your babes to safety. You know damn well Garbhan and Claudia will call Jeremy on any pig poo he flings. And, after what happened when Luc and Claudia lost their child, Nicholas would throw Jeremy in the Light gaol if he dared to give Chao a funny look."

"Actually, Chief Warden Nicolas would drag the acting high brother to Balance or Government House," Jonata said.

I looked at her. "Another contingency plan?"

She shrugged. "The Light wardens and staff are quite tired of piss-drunk seats. Brother Jeremy won't be able to self-medicate his pain this time."

I couldn't help it. I roared with laughter. Even Yin Li and Shi Hua giggled. At least, Jonata's jibe shook the future empress out of her melancholy.

I wiped away my own tears with my fingertips. "Shi Hua, please include me the next time you speak with High Brother Talbert."

"That's an abrupt change of subject." Yin Li's right eyebrow rose.

"Not really." I grinned. "Sister Migina of Conflict has expressed interest in doing her share of edict duty."

Shi Hua snorted. "She's upset Sister Zihna of Love hasn't had as much free time to spend with her since Zihna is expecting. Bedding Jeremy to make Zihna jealous is not wise."

"True," I admitted. "But Migina would definitely keep his mind off you wedding another man."

"Or make him too scared of ever laying with any woman ever again," Jonata commented.

We all looked at my warden.

"Is there a story you wish to share?" I asked sweetly.

Jonata glanced at the cabin door and lowered her voice. "Sister Migina took an interest in Long Feather during the Spring Rituals."

"I didn't know about this," I murmured.

"You and the other seats were busy with Crown Princess Chiara and Duke White Eagle." Jonata grinned. "He started hiding in the tunnels during his off hours. Until she trapped him down there."

"Trapped him?" Shi Hua's eyes were wide. "What did he do?"

"He told her while he thought she was attractive, he didn't dare cheat on the chief justice," Jonata finished.

Shi Hua and Yin Li burst out laughing.

"Oh, Balance." I ran my palms down my face. "No wonder she thought I was bedding anything that moved."

"What?" Yin Li said between hiccupping bursts of giggles.

I told them the story of our trip to Diné and Migina's attempts to have me bed every male in Conflict before she jumped to the assumption Claudia and I were lovers, which was her assumed reason I pouted about Claudia and Luc.

We laughed quite a bit more while we planned Shi Hua's trousseau. Part of me still wished Shi Hua were coming back to Issura with us, but I couldn't be selfish. I could follow her example though and perform my duties to the best of my ability.

Technically, any ordained member from all Twelve Temples could perform a wedding ceremony. Most couples preferred a priestess from Mother or Love as a symbol of family and commitment, but merchants preferred someone from Thief since their marriages were combined with business opportunities.

Over the next three days, we ripped apart the seams of Yin Li's Temple robes and reformed them into an appropriately-styled Jing wedding dress under her supervision. Little Squirrel and one of the female sailors volunteered to help us. Like Brother Hadar told to me so long ago onboard the *Unbridled*, sailors by their very trade needed to be nimble with both shears and needles.

According to Yin Li, red was the bridal color in their nation. Not that I saw colors the same way other humans did. But I could appreciate the style of a proper Jing noblewoman's dress.

Jonata carefully unraveled the gold thread from the badges on Shi Hua's Light uniforms. The Twelve must have known which supplies we would need. I bought cloth-of-gold ribbon and bleached linen from the trade goods the *Mars Tranquilus* carried. Titus only charged me enough to keep Duke Marco from firing him as the ship's captain.

When we finished the undergarments and wedding outfit, Shi Hua looked every inch like royalty. It was so different from the bare arms and flimsy dress she wore as Quan's alleged concubine the first time I met her.

For some reason, the impending nuptials aboard the *Mars Tranquilus* put everyone, crew and passengers, in a much lighter mood. We didn't have much in the way of a wedding feast beyond hard tack, lime marmalade, and jerky. However, the crew pooled their own coin to purchase one of the cases of Pana wine in the hold, their wedding gift to the future emperor and empress.

So on Sixth Day of our sixth week at sea, I performed the wedding ceremony of Bao Quan Po and Shi Hua on the main deck of the *Mars Tranquilus*. Luc stood as Quan's second. Yin Li performed the same service for her niece.

The day was warm without a cloud in the sky. The entire crew was topside to witness the ceremony, though a handful were manning the wheel and lines.

Everyone wore their best clothes, but by that point, we were all fairly odiferous after a month and a half at sea. I wore my formal chiton. Jonata assisted me with my hair, but this time, I asked her to let my braids cascade down my back.

Nerves assailed me when I stood below the quarterdeck with everyone staring at me. I had attended weddings before, but I'd never been the lead clergy. A silent prayer to Thief for his silver tongue and Knowledge to remember the entire ritual didn't settle my nerves or my upset stomach.

The hardtack and jerky truly aggravated my already disturbed digestive system. The healers' peppermint potion barely kept my nausea in check. I swallowed the lump at the back of my throat.

"We gather here today to celebrate the union of Bao Quan Po and Shi Hua." Somehow, I didn't stumble over any words until it was Shi Hua's turn to recite her vows.

Before she could utter a word, Quan looked her in the eye and blurted, "Last chance to back out, my dear."

She stuck out her tongue at him, and everyone laughed. Maybe we all needed a little jocularity.

"I swear to be faithful to you, Po. To support you no matter the trials we may face. And to care for and cherish our children that result from our union." Shi Hua actually looked . . . happy as recited her vows.

"Ambassador—" I took a deep breath and released it. "I mean, Po, please take Shi Hua's hand."

They held up their palms so that the pulse points at the base of their wrists touched, and they threaded the fingers of their right hands together.

I had draped the length of gold ribbon I'd retained from the spool for this ceremony over my shoulders. Concentrating on the twelve knots and the corresponding prayers, I took the ribbon and tied their hands and forearms together. When I stepped back, the muscles of my face were so tight I knew I was grinning like a fool.

"Before the Twelve and the witnesses, I pronounce you bound as wife and husband."

A cheer went up from the spectators. Quan gave Shi Hua a delicate peck on the lips, and her cheeks darkened to a deep red.

We didn't have sweet cakes or any other usual wedding dishes, but the wine was excellent, and everyone's shared joy made the day quite pleasant. The crew brought out their drums, and one of them had a Middle Sea double flute. I even danced a bit.

There was a great deal of teasing about Quan and Shi Hua not having any privacy on their wedding night until Luc suggested the storage room we'd been using to negotiate the marital contract. The crew immediately set to work to create a large pallet for the couple.

When they headed down the ladder, Quan's eyes met mine.

Don't make me regret marrying the two of you, I said silently.

I promise to treat my wife with all due respect, he replied. *I do not need either Shi Hua's or your blade between my ribs.*

As long as we understand each other, Your Highness.

Despite everyone's good mood, I couldn't help wondering if Shi Hua would have been better off if I beheaded her.

Chapter 24

After we retired to our cabin for the night, I asked Luc and our wardens for their suggestions in regards to Jeremy and his agitation over Shi Hua's wedding.

"With all due respect, m'lady, why do I have the feeling you already have a plan?" Long Feather said.

"I have a tentative idea, but I don't want to unleash Sister Migina on him unless it's absolutely necessary," I replied.

Jonata laughed, but all four men groaned.

I rolled to my side, leaned on my right elbow, and stared at Luc. "How many Light personnel did she accost?"

However, Yar answered first. "She can be rather aggressive."

Both Long Feather and Mateqai emitted sharp barks of laughter.

"That is an understatement." Luc's tone said he had been on the receiving end of Migina's attention.

"What happened?" I demanded.

"It's been a long day—" he started.

"High Brother, Sister Migina already thinks I ride everything alive thanks to a certain Balance warden," I said dryly.

"Jonata!" Long Feather roared.

"I thought the chief justice should know what happened to you before she sicced Sister Migina on Brother Jeremy," she shot back.

"Anthea, Sister Migina is an excellent Conflict priestess," Luc said.

"But her emotional intelligence when it comes to intimate relationships leaves something to be desired."

"Is this only in regards to certain genders?" I said. "Because Sister Zihna seems to find her satisfying in bed."

"All the Love clergy have to find their worshippers satisfactory in bed," Yar grumbled. "Regardless of their actual ability."

Jonata giggled, and Mateqai snickered.

"So who would be a good alternative to Migina for Jeremy?" I asked. "He's been infatuated with Shi Hua from the beginning. Surely, you know that."

"Jonata, Long Feather, does the chief justice meddle in the personal affairs of everyone in Balance, or does she merely single out Light for all this extra attention?" Luc said sourly.

"The truth?" Long Feather asked.

"Yes, please," Luc answered at the same time I protested, "I do not interfere in your lives!"

"Chief Justice, you didn't care about anyone until the night of the raid on Love." Long Feather's tone held no inflection, merely a statement of facts. "None of us blame you for your resentment on how the Reverend Mother handled your assignment to the Orrin Temple of Balance. But you blamed yourself for what happened to Warden Aglaia and High Brother Kam that night."

I swear my heart skipped a beat or two at Long Feather's words, but I had asked for the wardens' opinions of who could help Jeremy heal his broken heart.

"Their deaths weren't your fault," Long Feather continued. "You try to cover up your guilt by jesting whenever any of us volunteer for a duty outside of Balance. However, we all knew the potential dangers when we attended the Wardens Academy. You can't save us. It's our job to protect you. If Aglaia, Tyra, or Mylon were still here, they would tell you the same thing.

"So, to answer your question, High Brother, she interferes with all of us because she cares. More than she dares to admit."

It took me a few moments before I could trust myself to talk again. "That was a lovely speech, Warden, but it doesn't solve the problem of distracting Brother Jeremy from his broken heart."

"Instead of a priestess, what about Chief Warden Sabine?" Mateqai said.

Yar grunted. "I thought she was keeping company with Brother Keanu of Conflict."

"He got a little too serious for her taste," Jonata volunteered. "He wanted her to transfer to Conflict, but she refused. However, my understanding is their parting was amicable."

"I don't know." I lay down once again and snuggled into the crook of Luc's arm. "She seems rather serious for someone as young as Jeremy."

"Most people would say the same about you," Luc teased.

"Are you saying I should seduce Jeremy?" I shot back.

"I'm saying maybe Sabine needs someone to lighten her mood, Chief Justice," Luc said.

I smiled though none of them could see me. "I'll relay the suggestion to High Brother Talbert."

The next morning, I woke to the uncomfortable feeling of ants crawling all over my skin. I jerked upright and threw back my blankets, but there was nothing in the bed with me. In fact, all of the Issuran personnel were gone from our cabin.

I quickly dressed in my Temple uniform and robes. Since neither Jonata nor Luc were available, I pulled my braids back and tied them at the base of my neck with a leather thong.

The itching of my scalp was beginning to drive me insane. That was probably what really woke me. When we reached the Kingdom of

Ryukyu, I planned to soak in the hottest water available at the public baths for a whole day.

Nausea added to my disagreeable feeling. I took another dose of Master Bly's digestive remedy. I'd been on ships many times. This voyage was different from the rest only in terms of length. Maybe Sivan was right. Maybe I was experiencing the physical aftermath of all the stress I had been under for the last year and a half.

When I stepped out of our cabin, warmth caressed my face. It was another clear day. The crew and the other passengers laughed and joked. Obvious betting was going on until they noticed I was on the deck. Quan and Shi Hua were the only people missing.

I crossed to where Luc was perched on an equipment box and sat down next to him. "Should I tell them, or have you already placed your wager?"

"Already place my wager," he mumbled around a mouthful of venison jerky from the smell. "Want some?" He held out a small bag.

I held up my hand and swallowed hard at the odor. "No, thank you."

"You don't have a hangover." His concern caressed my psyche. "You only had a couple sips of your wine after the wedding. Are you picking up on Huizhong's motion sickness?"

"This started a week or two before we boarded the *Mars Tranquilus*," I murmured. "Neither Master Bly nor Master Devin could find anything physically wrong with me. Sivan thinks my ill feeling is my body's reaction to working through all the mental and emotional stress since I was assigned to the seat of Balance."

"Did you consult with Mya?" Luc asked.

"I didn't have a chance to before we had to leave," I admitted.

He frowned at me. "We need to consult with a healer when we reach Ryukyu. I'm also worried about after effects from your poisoning."

The renegades had poisoned the Orrin Healers Guild's sweet almond oil supply. It had been their backup plan when the assassin failed to slit my throat on the steps of Light. Or Luc could have been referring to the cursed demon grimoire that nearly sucked me into their web. Either way, there were more than enough physical reasons for me to still be feeling ill.

I nodded. "It wouldn't hurt to get another opinion."

His frown deepened, but he remained silent.

"What?" I demanded.

"I know something's really wrong when you don't argue with me about seeing a healer," he said.

I stuck my tongue out at him, but I couldn't disagree with him.

Before either of us could continue our discussion, Little Squirrel called out from the crow's nest. "Captain, ships dead ahead."

Chapter 25

◆

I jumped off the equipment box and fumbled with the ties of my robes.

"Colors?" Titus shouted back.

Little Squirrel peered through her distance-viewer to confirm her sighting. "No flags. No sails. Four vessels. Langskips!" She tucked the strap of the distance-viewer over her chest in preparation to climb down.

"Stay up in the nest!" Titus spotted me. "Get your priestesses up in the forecastle, m'lady!"

"Aye, Captain!" I responded. *Shi Hua, Yin Li, I need you and your bows up on the forecastle now!*

Your timing couldn't possibly be worse, Quan grumbled at the back of my mind.

Blame it on the skinwalkers, I retorted.

I tore off my robes as I ran to our cabin. While I could normally fight in them, they would weigh me down if I fell overboard.

A shudder ran through me. Was that how my grandmother died during the Battle of Orrin Bay nearly thirty years ago? Had she been weighted down by her clothing and weapons? Or worse, weighted down and drowned by ship debris? What even brought up that thought?

But I didn't have time to examine the idea further. Not with skinwalkers rowing straight toward the *Mars Tranquilus.*

132

Yin Li burst out of the captain's cabin, her son on her heels. "But, Mother, I can help!" he wailed.

"I—" The Love priestess spotted me and gave me a pleading look.

"Yin Shang, I need your assistance," I said. The boy immediately brightened. "Please aid in protecting the crown prince. Four guards will not be sufficient if the enemy boards the *Mars Tranquilus*."

He frowned. "But I know archery!"

"I have no doubt of your proficiency, sir." I knelt next to him. "But you're the only one of Conflict blood we have on board. My mission is to get Prince Po back to Jing, and I need your help to accomplish that mission."

Yin Shang nodded sharply. "I understand, Chief Justice. But he's not in the cabin, so I should go to where he is."

"The other guards are bringing him here as we speak, so I need you to keep the cabin secure until they arrive." I smiled. "Retrieve your bow and quiver, and be ready."

"Yes, Chief Justice." He straightened his little spine and marched back into the cabin.

Thank you, Yin Li said silently.

You're welcome. I smiled at her before I entered the passenger cabin.

The door slammed open as I kicked off my boots. Luc entered, followed by our wardens. "We're coming with you," he announced as the five of them gathered their own weapons.

"But—" I started.

"We cannot put the Crown Prince's wife at risk," Yar said. "She will stay low, and Mateqai will cover her while she charges arrows for the rest of us."

"But Luc—" I tried again.

"I'll do the same thing as Shi Hua," he said. "The *Mars Tranquilus* doesn't have a catapult on the forecastle. If you can ward us and Sister Yi Li can do the same for the catapult crew on the aftcastle, we have a Thief's chance of getting out of this intact."

I hated he was right about the odds. We needed to be faster and smarter than the skinwalkers. They had the raw numbers of talent on their side, and they'd be ready for the same tricks we performed in our last encounter.

Once we were armed, I informed Titus of the change in tactics verbally while relaying them silently to Yin Li. Instead of bristling over my usurpation of the defense of his ship, he nodded.

"Then no evasive maneuvers?" he asked.

I grinned. "Straight ahead with as much speed as you can muster. Under normal circumstances, I'd lay my gold on you, your crew, and your ship. But with demon-damned opponents, we needed to take the offensive."

Behind Titus, Quan's guards hustled him toward his cabin. The prince turned toward me and yelled, "You'd better keep my wife alive, Anthea!"

"Yes, Your Highness!" I hollered back. While I scrambled up the steps to the forecastle, I said a prayer to Thief for a little extra luck defending the *Mars Tranquilus* and the lives of those aboard. Unsurprisingly, He remained as silent as Balance.

"Long Feather, you're with Sister Yin Li on the aftcastle to shield the catapult and crew." There was no reason to avoid the priestess's title any longer. The entire crew knew she was Temple after our last encounter with the skinwalkers.

He nodded and raced after Yin Li.

Luc and Shi Hua sat behind the spare line boxes on each side of the forecastle. Yar and Mateqai stood with their respective clergy as Luc and Shi Hua charged arrows and crossbow bolts. Unfortunately, they had to place a separate spell on each projectile. If the charging spell was placed on a collection of arrows or bolts, the spell expired as soon as on was plucked from the pile.

Sea Wolf double-checked that all of us were harnessed and our lines securely tied to the ship before he donned his own harness. "We come to serve, m'lady."

His acknowledgement of my leadership in defense of the ship added another level of weight to my shoulders. The langskips approached faster than I would have preferred. Like before, the painful itch of demon magic came from the four sorcerers at the center of the lead langskip. If we managed to slip by the four ships, we would buy a few precious moments for the catapult crew to launch sea fire at their sterns.

I wasn't as proficient with a bow as I was with a sword. It came from learning both when I had been totally blind. A sword extended my reach. A bow depended on the accuracy of my hearing. But with a Balance spell, an arrow's accuracy wasn't as important. Since I used time itself as a weapon, a glancing blow would discharge the spell. And now, I could actually see my target.

The lead langskip aimed for the *Mars Tranquilus*'s bow, their intention to ram us clear. I blew out a deep breath to calm my jittery nerves.

"Ready!" I drew the bowstring back to my ear. The sailors on either side of me did the same.

"Aim!" I focused on the four skinwalkers anchored to the mast.

"Fire!" The barrage of Light-charged arrows and bolts masked my Balance spell.

The skinwalkers focused on warding their rowers, not the langskip itself. My arrow struck a plank right above the water line. The spell discharged, and the wood rotted at an accelerated rate.

I grabbed my next arrow and charged it with Balance magic. "Ready!"

The first langskip listed to the right of the *Mars Tranquilus*. "Aim!"

Confusion reigned on the langskip as the skinwalkers realized they were in trouble.

"Fire!" I roared. The flight of arrows arched over the water. This time, the Light-charged projectiles struck several of the oarsmen and one of the sorcerers. My own arrow struck the plank below the water-line. The wood disintegrated. Shouts erupted from the skinwalkers.

"Five degrees to port!" Titus roared. The crew adjusted the sails as the captain turned the wheel. We avoided the foundering langskip, but we still faced their three sisters ahead.

Yin Li, make sure the langskip passing on our starboard sinks.

It will be my pleasure, the Love priestess answered.

I slung my bow over my shoulder. We weren't going to take the other langskips by surprise. The burning, itchy sensation of demon magic warned me, and I threw up my wards.

Luc and Shi Hua fed their energy into me. Together, we kept the destructive spells from obliterating the bow of the *Mars Tranquilus*.

A cheer went up from the stern. *The first langskip is burning underwater, and we're picking off the surviving skinwalkers*, Yin Li reported.

You'll have a second target on the port side in a moment. I shifted my attention to Titus. *Captain, I need you to resume your original course.*

We'll hit the second langskip, m'lady, he replied.

No, we won't.

Titus was silent for a moment before he said, *I'm not the one who will owe the duke a new ship.*

Look at it this way. Neither of us will have to answer to him if I'm wrong.

Titus's laughter could be heard all over the ship before he shouted orders. The crew scurried to set the sails for the next course change.

"Sea Wolf, take command of the archers," I barked.

"Aye, Lady Justice!"

I concentrated on the approaching langskip and froze it in time. Sea waves flowed around the keel. The enemy ship's oars hung between one stroke and the next.

The strain on my mind and body was incredible, but if I failed, Titus was right. We'd hit the langskip, and everyone aboard the *Mars*

Tranquilus would die. It didn't matter if the cause were by drowning, shark, or our enemies skinning us alive.

Demon magic fought against my spell, but with the skinwalkers frozen along with their ship, the sensation was more akin to a poison oak rash than the awful rasp of their full power. Luc and Shi Hua poured more energy into me. So much energy, I feared the odd prickle of lightning on the edge of my power. If this first trick worked, maybe, just maybe, I could call a controlled lightning strike on the other two langskips.

But it was an awfully big maybe.

My tunic grew damp, whether from perspiration or sea spray didn't matter. The annoying itch of the skinwalkers attempts to break my time spell grew into an uncomfortable heat. I gritted my teeth and tightened my grip on the time lines. This was nothing compared to what Elizabeth went through when she had been held prisoner and tortured in her own gaol cells. Or when Bertrice held the final resort spells of Death in Tandor. I could hold the other ship.

I had to hold the langskip.

"Ready! Aim! Fire!" Sea Wolf barked.

The Light-charged arrows simply stopped a yard short of the time-frozen langskip.

"Ready!" the pilot bellowed again.

Hold. Everyone on the forecastle stand down. Everyone heard Luc's silent voice. *Sister Yin Li, is the catapult ready?*

Yes, High Brother.

Luc was right. We needed to conserve our ammunition. *On my command,* he added.

With the strong trade winds, the *Mars Tranquilus* whipped past the langskip. *Launch!* Luc ordered.

The deck thrummed beneath my bare feet with the force of the catapult's release. I dropped my spell when I felt Yin Li raise her wards to protect the catapult crew.

Screams of pain mixed with shouts of anger and frustration from behind us while another cheer rose from the catapult crew. I unhooked my harness, ran to the starboard side of the forecastle, and leaned over the railing.

Yin Li's shield turned out to be unnecessary. The jar of sea fire hit dead center of the langskip. Pink-white flames rose around the mast, and the skinwalkers howled as they burned. More arrows flew from the stern of the *Mars Tranquilus* and quieted the screams.

Demon magic rasped along my skin, not from the stern. I whirled and raced back to my position. Sea Wolf reattached the line to my harness.

"What's the next Temple trick you plan to show them?" He grinned wildly behind his blue beard.

"The next one will be a trick," I muttered. "The trick will be not killing everyone on the *Mars Tranquilus* in the process."

"You can't be serious!" Luc said behind me. "Are you trying to do the skinwalkers' work for them by calling lightning?"

Chapter 26

I wasn't sure why I was surprised. Of course, Luc had heard my thoughts. Our bond went far beyond any other relationship I'd ever had.

I turned to find him kneeling on the forecastle and staring at me over the line box. So was Shi Hua.

"It worked with the two wechuges last summer," I retorted.

"I was there!" Shi Hua looked at me as if I'd lost all the acorns in my skull Mya had oh-so-carefully replaced. "We were damn lucky you didn't burn down the entire block!"

"There's only the four of us with talent—" I started.

"Pardon me?" Sea Wolf protested.

I glared at the pilot. "What is your strategy? Map the skinwalkers away?"

He huffed. "Just because I'm not Temple doesn't mean I am not talented."

"While you two are arguing semantics, we have two ships full of skinwalkers headed straight for us!" Luc yelled.

"Then pass the word that everyone needs to take cover!" I yelled back.

Luc passed the warning through silent speech, but Titus emphasized the command out loud, including Little Squirrel in the crow's nest.

All personnel are lower than the masts and the aftcastle, Luc reported.

I glanced at my companions on the forecastle. They knelt or crouched below the railing, though they kept their bows and crossbows at the ready. I returned my attention to the approaching langskips.

The odd prickle of power surged through me as I concentrated on our foes. Neither Temple magic nor demon magic, it was more like the energy the Wildlings released when they shifted into their animal forms. If I survived this voyage, I would need to ask High Brother Jax about the power.

Despite my initial reservations, I focused on drawing that odd energy like I had when we needed to destroy the bodies of the two wechuges. The mother and daughter had been transformed into predators of magic and ice from their cannibalism. Simply melting their bodies was insufficient. We had to boil away their remains faster than they could reform.

However, when I used lightning to destroy the wechuges, I was under the influence of the dead demons that formed the alien grimoire. I prayed the Twelve wouldn't hold that incident against me.

White-hot light sparkled along my arms and hands. Clouds gathered above us, and the waves grew choppy. The *Mars Tranquilus* sped faster toward the enemy with the increased winds.

"Steady, people! Steady!" Titus called out.

The two langskips aimed straight for us.

I thrust out my palms and release the energy. White light enveloped the entire world. The *Mars Tranquilus* shuddered beneath my bare feet. I blinked in an effort to clear the spots and tears from my eyes.

A blast of water, wind and magic backlash slammed into me. I flew backward. The line snapped, and my spine and ribs crashed into something hard and unyielding. The landing on the deck knocked any remaining air out of my lungs. I fought to draw a breath.

Ignoring the agony in my chest, I carefully rolled onto my back and wiped sea water from my face. Black spots danced in my vision, but I could make out the bloody orb of the sun between the sails. The oddest part was the laughter.

Human laughter, not the queer chitter-cough of demons.

"You still with us, Chief Justice?" Little Squirrel crouched next to me.

"Did it work?" I rasped. The taste of smoke filled my mouth, and it felt like I'd blasted my own innards. "Did the lightning strike both langskips?"

"Yes, m'lady." Her hands reached for me, but she stopped herself. "May I touch you, m'lady? To check for injuries?"

"Yes." I closed my eyes and tried to relax. My very muscles threatened to spasm and contract like they had in the Valley of the Lost last fall when I froze hundreds of square leagues of a flash flood to save Brother Sisquoc. More hands touched my body, searching for injuries.

"The brain injury's been there since I've known her," Luc grumbled from above me.

I opened my eyes to find Jonata kneeling on my right. Luc hovered over both women.

"Are the skinwalkers dead?" Ash seemed to coat my talents as well as my skin and mouth.

"An entire barrel of Jing flash powder couldn't have done as much damage as you did," he teased.

"Little Squirrel!" Titus bellowed. "Quit pretending to be a healer! Get your arse back up to the crow's nest!"

"Aye, captain!" The sailor winked at me before she scrambled for the main mast.

"I'm all right, Jonata." I tried to rise, but she pressed a spot on my side. The pain made me cry out.

"That's what I was afraid of," she murmured. "You've cracked at least one rib, but more likely it's three."

I choked back a sob while she continued to touch the area. "Then please stop poking my broken bones."

"Ming Wei whined less when she fell off Nassa," Jonata said dryly.

My pain faded at my shock and worry over the Balance squire. "When did this happen?"

Jonata lowered her already soft voice. "While Child was caring for you. She only acquired a few bruises and scrapes."

"Balance," I swore. "Can everyone in our Temple try to make it through a season without any injuries or deaths?"

"Be thankful Thief protects you lot," Luc snapped. "You barely missed a taut line that would have decapitated you."

I looked at him. "I am thankful. More than you know."

"Then let's get you back to your cabin, and get those ribs wrapped." Shi Hua stood near my feet. "We're going to have to find you a healer when we reach Ryukyu."

Sea Wolf appeared next to . . . the empress. I needed to beat her change in position into my head. It wouldn't do to address her informally or by the wrong title when we reach Jing.

"High Brother, Your Highness, why don't the two of you step out of the way, and let me and the warden do the heavy lifting?" Sea Wolf said.

"Heavy lifting?" I knew I looked as perturbed as I felt.

"No offense offered, m'lady." The pilot laughed heartily. "Personally, I respect a woman who knows real work rather than the noble daughters who prowl the docks."

I was sure there was another word he would have used instead of "respect" if Shi Hua weren't standing next to him. However, she and Luc moved out of the way.

Jonata and Sea Wolf helped me to my feet. I gritted my teeth against the agonizing process. No doubt my entire body would be covered in hot red bruises by First Evening.

"Let's get you to our cabin, Chief Justice." Jonata tried to steer me in that direction.

"No, I need to see the langskips."

Thank Balance, neither she nor Sea Wolf argued with me. My knees and ribs complained as we climbed the steps to the forecastle. I needed the ship's rail to stay upright.

Ahead of the *Mars Tranquilus's* bow, thick yellow smoke rose from the wood floating on the surface. The gray-green corpses were turning blue as the sea sucked the remaining heat from them. I counted the Twelve's blessings that demon magic no longer rasped against my mental shields.

"Balance picked the right time to make sure you controlled this new talent of yours," Luc murmured at my right shoulder.

"And I managed not to destroy the *Mars Tranquilus.*" I chuckled until the agony in my chest became too much. "Which is a good thing because I certainly don't have the gold to reimburse Duke Marco."

Titus ordered our course altered so we sailed around the wreckage instead of through it. A wise move since the skinwalkers may have left trap spells in the debris. Nor did we need a floating ember setting our own ship ablaze.

Once we were clear, I said, "I think I'm ready for—"

"Captain!" Little Squirrel shouted from her lookout. "More ships on the horizon!"

My muscles tensed painfully as I waited for Little Squirrel's bad news. We were still a day away from encountering local ships from the islands and nations of the Old Continent.

"Four—no, five ships to the southwest of our position." She paused a moment. "Three ships to the northwest."

Exhaustion and pain made my steps falter as I approached the railing on the port side of the bow. Please, Thief, don't let there be more skinwalkers.

"The five vessels to the southwest are langskips, Captain!" Little Squirrel reported.

The lead ship crested over a wave. Telltale gray-green lined the side of the vessel and surrounded the base of the mast.

My heart hammered. We might be able to take out one or two of the langskips with sea fire. The archers still had a number of arrows and bolts charged with Light magic, but they would have to get past the sorcerers warding the ships.

I turned to look at Luc. He scowled at the oncoming enemy before he met my gaze.

The trick will be pulling some insane idea out of our arses, he joked silently.

You've been corrupted by being in my company for far too long, I replied.

Maybe the demons broke me last summer, but a part of me suspected Luc and I would die fighting side-by-side.

"Northwest are two chuan accompanied by a third ship I don't recognize!" Little Squirrel shouted from the crow's nest. "It looks like a modified, larger caravel!"

A glimmer of hope filled me, and I hobbled to the starboard side as fast as my aching legs could carry my carcass.

"Mind your stations!" Titus roared from his position at the wheel.

The very human deep yellow and bright orange figures darted around on the deck of the lead ship of the second group. But it was the four green masts that shot relief through me. Maybe Thief had listened to my pleas after all.

"It's the *Unbridled*!" I shouted. "We have help from Jing!"

Chapter 27

A cheer rose from the crew and passengers aboard the *Mars Tranquilus.*

Reverend Fathers Jin and Biming are onboard the Unbridled. Shi Hua pulled Yin Li, Luc, and me into their conversation.

Anthea, have your captain alter course for our fleet so we can cover the Mars Tranquilus, Reverend Father Biming ordered.

I relayed the command to Titus. It amazed me how men could grunt an acknowledgement in silent speech. Titus shouted to his crew. Sails and lines shifted to allow the ship to race towards our defenders.

The deck tilted as we made the turn, and I clung to the railing. However, we weren't safe yet by any means. We were still outnumbered.

Demon magic stung my skin. All five langskips were full of sorcerers. While I had no doubt the three Jing ships were full of Temple personnel and experienced sailors, how many of them had faced demons or skinwalkers?

Most of us were in Chengzhou when the demons attacked the palace and Temple, Reverend Father Biming chided.

"Captain, the enemy ships have raised sails!" Little Squirrel reported.

The wind abruptly shifted. Our sails sagged as the breeze came from the south. The langskips poured on speed to intercept us before we reached the Jing ships. Balance help us! They had a wind talent at the very least. I prayed the sorcerer in question wasn't a weather wizard as well.

Titus bellowed more orders. The booms of the *Mars Tranquilus* shifted to catch the southern gusts. Meanwhile the Jing vessels had to adjust their tacking maneuvers to make any headway.

"I don't suppose you can call lightning again, can you?" Sea Wolf loaded a charged bolt into his crossbow.

"Twelve help us, it was a wonder she stayed conscious this time," Luc grumbled.

"I don't remember flying across Mistress Jaci's courtyard when we battled the wechuges," I retorted.

"Because you weren't conscious," Luc shot back.

I chose to ignore his comment. "I can ward while you and Shi Hua charge arrows and bolts."

"Yin Li and the catapult crew will be taking the brunt of the next attack," he said.

He and I looked at each other as we recognized the danger.

"Shi Hua! Stay here and help Sea Wolf!" I jabbed a forefinger at the deck of the forecastle.

A surge of adrenaline took the edge off my pain as I followed Luc to the steps. I held his crutches while he hopped down. Yar protested with a growl, which I ignored. I handed the crutches to Luc and scrambled after him. Yar and Jonata followed us.

Should we stash the prince in the hold? If a demon spell gets by me—

Luc swore a colorful Cantan oath and swerved toward the captain's cabin. He knocked and waited for one of Quan's guards to answer. No sense accidentally getting run through with a spear.

Thankfully, Huizhong answered the door. Luc relayed the situation. "Get the prince down in the empty hold."

The Jing guard laughed. "You mean the one we just pulled him out of."

Yin Shang ducked under Huizhong's arm. "Do not worry, High Brother. We will ensure the crown prince's safety."

Thankfully, both men controlled their impulse to laugh.

"I am grateful I can depend on your service, Yin Shang." I inclined my head. "But please hurry, I fear the enemy will catch up with us before the Jing fleet does."

"Understood," Huizhong and Yin Shang said at the same time. Luc and I continued up to the aftcastle with me biting my tongue to keep from laughing myself or screaming in pain. The Temple of Conflict wouldn't know what struck them when that boy became a novice.

The view from the stern immediately sobered me. The langskips were closing in on the *Mars Tranquilus*.

Yin Li stepped closer. "Thank you for the reinforcement. I wasn't sure I could ward against five full ships of skinwalkers."

Jonata knelt in front of me to remove the end of broken line from the buckles of my harness. Meanwhile, Yar assisted Luc in sitting behind the storage box, out of the line of fire. He immediately started charging the arrows and bolts of the aft defenders.

I looked at the box holding the jars of sea fire. It burned in water, but oils floated on top of water—

"Wardens! With me!" I turned and scrambled back down the stairs to the main deck. Titus yelled for Little Squirrel to get her arse out of the crow's nest as I ran past him. Huizhong stood by the opening to the below decks.

"Don't close the hatch!" My breath came in great gasps as I slid to a stop. "We need a couple of barrels of oil from below."

Little Squirrel joined us. "We'll need a little extra help to get barrels topside."

"My comrades can help." Huizhong smirked. "I'm sure Master Yin Shang can protect the crown prince for a few moments while we assist you."

"Thank you. I am sure he can handle such duties." I grinned back.

Little Squirrel scampered down the ladder. I climbed down, and

Huizhong followed me, He barked out orders in Jing, and the adult guards join us. Little Squirrel showed us where the barrels of oil were stored. Quan and Yin Shang watched us from the doorway to the smaller storage room while we rolled three barrels down the aisle.

I nearly passed out because I couldn't take a deep breath. We didn't have time to deal with my injuries. The pain reminded me what was at stake.

Netting already lay on the deck planks. Under Little Squirrel's direction, the wardens and sailors on the main deck hauled the first barrel up and through the hatch. Since they didn't need me for a moment, I leaned against the wall of the small storage room in order to stay upright.

"Are we resorting to throwing trade goods at the skinwalkers?" Quan quipped. But the greenish cast to his skin told me his true feelings far better than reading his thoughts. I couldn't blame him after what happened to us in Tandor. I had no intention of being chained and helpless again. But I also hadn't been tortured like he had been, though the skinwalker who had possessed High Brother Dav had every intention of doing the same to me.

"If I have to." I glanced at the second barrel rising toward the hatch before I turned back to him and grinned. "At the rate I'm going, I will empty the entire Balance treasury to get you home. But you will be out of my hair, Your Highness. This, I swear."

His color shifted back to his normal orange-ish yellow, and he smiled in return. "Of your intentions and your abilities, I have no doubt, Chief Justice."

"Are you truly using the catapult to launch the barrels at the enemy ships?" Little Yin Shang's expression was so earnest.

"Not exactly. After the ships chasing us have been taken care of, I promise to explain everything to you."

"But—"

"Issura and Jing have both had too many problems with spies, Master Yin Shang," Quan said gently. "The chief justice is wise to keep her plans to herself." He looked directly at me. "And if she makes a promise to you, she will keep it, no matter the cost."

If he meant to reassure me, he failed. I knew all too well the high costs others paid for my decisions.

The last barrel disappeared through the hatch. One of the crew called down, "Clear!"

"Until later, good sirs." I nodded to Quan and Yin Shang before I followed Little Squirrel up the ladder. The climb up was agony compared to the climb down. Getting lashed for insubordination again would have been preferable.

Thankfully, the warden and crew hauled the barrels up to the aftcastle.

"What next?" Little Squirrel asked.

"Toss them overboard," I said. "One to port, one to starboard, and one straight off the stern."

The crew literally glowed at my orders. It was reassuring they could read my intentions the same way my wardens did. I got very tired of explaining myself over and over.

Yin Li stepped closer. *Are you all right, Anthea? You look like you're on the verge of passing out.*

No, I'm not all right, but we'll deal with my injuries after we've taken care of the skinwalkers.

Aloud I shouted, "Archers, make sure you have charged arrows and bolts, but wait for my signal."

Yin Li and five of the sailors prepared their weapons. The wardens and crew worked together to throw the barrels into the sea.

Stepping up to the railing, I ordered, "Now!"

The archers launched their arrows and bolts. I whispered the spell to freeze time around the barrels the instant they were struck.

We continued sailing north. I couldn't breathe properly. My limbs shook. Sweat ran down my face and torso. My fingernails dug into the wood of the railing.

But I had to hold my spell until the last possible instant.

Shouts from the langskips traveled across the water the moment the skinwalkers sensed my spell. They started to alter their course. I released the frozen time.

The spell-heated oil barrels exploded.

Chapter 28

The waves spread the burning oil across the surface of the sea. The lead langskip sailed straight into the pink flames. The second tried to reverse course, but the oars cut through the oil and dragged the fire back to them. The langskip on the far left and the two on the right tacked to evade the inferno.

My plan bought the *Mars Tranquilus* a few precious moments. The small Jing fleet sailed by us. Another cheer rose from the personnel on our ship. There were answering salutes, but the majority focused on the langskips.

Human magic tingled along my skin, giving me a small measure of energy. Yin Li laid her hand on mine, and she fed me a measure of her power to blunt the pain in my body as we watched the now evenly matched fleets.

Hot white fire flared on the forward decks of the carrack and the two chuan. Spell-enhanced rockets whistled through toward the three surviving langskips. A few of the missiles missed the enemy ships, but the majority exploded on the decks. Howls of pain trailed off as the magic did its work.

The rough touch of demon spells rasped along my skin. Wards went up around the three Jing ships.

"Yin Li—"

The Love priestess caught the warning in my tone. Her wards

enveloped the stern of the *Mars Tranquilus*. Luc added his power to hers.

I couldn't muster the energy to block the thoughts and emotions of the people around me, much less throw up a basic ward. All I could do was cling to the railing and watch the battle.

One of the langskips swung around the outermost chuan. Fear and worry ran through the passengers and crew of our ship. The chuan and the carrack couldn't maneuver as fast as the langskips. We were all too dependent on the wind. Demon magic-enhanced skinwalker rowers provided the langskips with a majority of their velocity.

The sorcerers at the mast each threw a plasma bolt at us. Yin Li cried out as she deflected the demon-tinged magic. We were in trouble again.

Big trouble.

But how could we stop them?

We filter our power through your skills, Luc, Yin Li, and Shi Hua chorused inside my head.

I can't hold off another barrage by myself, Yin Li said.

I've already told High Brother Zhu our plan, Shi Hua added. *They are preparing their rockets.*

You can do this, my love, Luc whispered.

I realized the three of them were absorbing my pain so I could focus on casting the time freeze spell. I took a deep breath, and let my rage at all the harm these self-absorbed, idiotic, bootlickers had caused.

And I whispered the spell.

Scarlet spots danced in my vision, but I clung to the time-frozen langskip. Demon magic clawed at my mind as the sorcerers tried to free themselves. I couldn't block them and keep ahold of the spell.

Love filled me, driving away the rage. It lifted and supported me. Nor did the feeling come solely from Yin Li. Luc's deeper feelings. And . . . Shi Hua?

My surprise at the depth of her emotions for me nearly made me release the spell. Her laughter tinkled like a bell inside my psyche.

What? You think Po is the only person enamored with you? Hold tight. The Feiyun *is about to launch their rockets.*

The threads of time started to slip through my fingers, the urge to move forward more powerful than any river. My body shook in earnest. Jonata and Little Feather's solid grips on my arms were the reason I was still upright.

Let go, Anthea.

I did as Shi Hua said. I freed time. My fingers relaxed. The red spots in my vision turned white.

And I fell into the blinding light.

Chapter 29

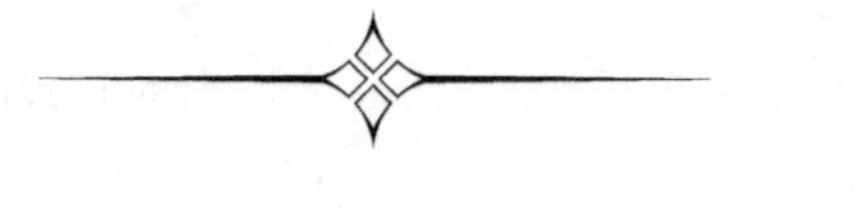

An obnoxious smell, worse than cat urine, yanked me out of the white pit intent on swallowing me. I jerked away from the odor, which launched a round of agony in my chest.

"She's awake." Luc's callused palm held my left hand. "The skinwalker's last spell—"

"I'm . . . fine." It was difficult to talk when I could only take small sips of air. "Not . . . demon . . . magic. Over . . . extended . . . myself."

Luc clicked his tongue against his teeth but refrained from saying anything out loud or silently. He released my hand, pushed himself upright on his crutches, and moved out of the way.

I gritted my own teeth, but I couldn't stop the grunts of pain when Long Feather and Yar hauled me to my feet. Above us, the *Mars Tranquilus*'s sails had been partially lowered.

"Why—"

"Shi Hua's coordinating between the four ships," Luc said.

Shi Hua.

Her revelation of her feelings left me heartbroken. I didn't return her love. I couldn't return her love. The last thing I ever wanted to do was to cause her any pain. This was even worse than the situation between me and Claudia. If Luc or Yin Li heard what Shi Hua had told me, they said nothing about it. But then, neither one would do so would in front of this many witnesses.

Twelve help me, did Quan know about his wife's affections for me?

While the wardens assisted me down the steps from the aftcastle, the *Unbridled* maneuvered to take the lead of our little flotilla. The two chuan covered the *Mars Tranquilus*'s stern. Once all the vessels were in position, Titus ordered full sail again. The deaths of the skinwalkers had obliterated the unnatural breeze from the south. Balance set the trade winds to their normal pattern, and we headed west. For the first time since we left Orrin, I felt we had a better than zero chance of returning Quan home alive.

When my escort reached the passenger cabin and helped me to mine and Luc's bed, the women took over. Yin Li ordered the two male wardens out, and she closed the door. Jonata and Little Squirrel undressed me while Yin Li attempted to block my pain, though her resources were as nearly exhausted as my own.

The warden and the sailor used clean strips of bandages to tightly wrap the cracked bones in my chest. Jonata did a second check to make sure there wasn't any other broken bits of my skeleton floating around inside me.

"The Twelve are going to make you pay for pushing yourself like this, m'lady," Jonata murmured.

"Mind your tongue, Warden," Yin Li snapped.

"Warden Jonata is right," Little Squirrel bit back.

"Stop. All of you." The need to take a deeper breath warred with the pain in my chest. "Sister, I've asked my wardens to give me their honest analysis. And I hate to admit it, but Jonata is right. Thank the Twelve, Reverend Father Biming arrived with plenty of Temple assistance."

"I apologize for overstepping my place, Chief Justice, Warden Jonata." Yin Li bowed to both of us.

"Apology accepted," I said. "Obviously, Crown Prince Po and his lady wife haven't explained how unconventional Orrin's Temple of Balance is."

Both Jonata and Little Squirrel laughed as they tied off the bandages.

"I have medicines in my kit," Yin Li murmured. "Including soma tears."

"Thank you for your offer, Sister." Jonata crossed her arms and eyed me. "Are you going to cooperate with us, or do I need to have Long Feather and Yar hold you down to take a couple of soma tears?"

"How about an alternative?" I smiled. "Pain powder for now. And I'll take the soma tears before retiring for the night. If I have any organ injuries, I don't want to sleep through my death."

"That's acceptable, m'lady." Jonata smiled in return.

"You are all mad." Yin Li shook her head. None of us disputed her.

She and Little Squirrel helped me into my sleep tunic and propped me against the cabin wall using several pillows Yin Li appropriated from her cabin. Meanwhile, Jonata mixed pain powder in a goblet with Pana red.

When she brought me the silver cup, I looked inside before I looked at her. "You know how to ruin good wine, Warden."

"Would you prefer the soma tears?" The implicit threat in her mild tone said she would have no problem getting Long Feather to hold me while pouring the drug down my throat. In my current state though, the tiny woman didn't need her taller counterpart's assistance.

I downed the red wine in two gulps and scrunched my face at the bitter aftertaste. I held out the cup. "May I please have some unadulterated Pana red?"

Jonata smiled. "Yes, m'lady."

At the knock on the cabin door, Little Squirrel opened it a crack and whispered to someone.

"I'm not dying. Let them in." My command would have sounded more impressive if I could take a full breath and not wheeze like an elderly woman with phthisis.

Luc swung in on his crutches. "The crown prince wants us to attend him while he speaks with Reverend Fathers Biming and Jin. Are you sure you're up to this, Anthea?"

A wry smile twisted my mouth. "I suspected they would want our perspective. Warden Jonata was smart enough not to slip soma tears in my wine. Can we have this discussion in our cabin though? These women worked very hard to make me reasonably comfortable."

"The crown prince graciously suggested we accommodate your comfort." Luc tried very hard not to grin, but the corners of his lips tilted upward.

Jonata handed me the refilled cup. "Long Feather and I will be right outside if you need us, m'lady."

"Thank you." I saluted her with the cup. "To all of you."

"Let her get some rest after your conference, High Brother." Little Squirrel nodded to Luc as she departed. Surprisingly, Jonata didn't say anything else when she followed the second officer out of the cabin.

"What was that all about?" Luc crossed the cabin to perch at the foot of our shared bed.

"That was an example of Little Bear and Gina's training of Balance's newest wardens," I replied.

"Do you always allow such insubordination, Lady Justice?" Yin Li asked.

Before I could answer, Luc burst out laughing. "She tells them to be honest with her, and then constantly threatens to lash the wardens and staff when they are, but they know she won't do it."

"Because you were lashed?" Yin Li asked softly.

I sighed. Of course, she had seen the scars on my back. Maybe Reverend Mother Alara's overly strict adherence to Temple rules was why I was so lenient with my people.

"I believe the punishment should be commiserate with the crime as well as the cause of the crime."

She nodded thoughtfully. "That is Justice Men Wei's view as well. Maybe when this war is over, more justices will adapt that concept."

Quan opened the cabin door and ushered Shi Hua inside. His wife, I reminded myself. I married the couple—

Balance help me, was it only yesterday morning?

Why did I even care about what Shi Hua said? I loved Luc. We'd been through too much together, depended on each other—

And our relationship had all been part of the Reverend Mother's manipulation of me.

What if Shi Hua was doing the same on behalf of her husband? Or worse, on his orders?

"How are you, Anthea?" She looked at me with such concern.

"Worse than when I was lashed. Better than when I was poisoned," I said dryly.

Quan scowled, but he didn't say a word. No doubt I would hear his commentary on the subject the next time we were alone.

"She didn't want to take soma tears until after our discussion with the Reverend Fathers," Yin Li offered. "But please, Your Highness, don't extend the conversation longer than necessary.

Shi Hua turned to Quan. "My aunt is right. I want Anthea's opinion as much as you do, but we need to make this conference quick so she can get some rest."

"All four of you need a respite," Quan said. "We still have no idea where these langskips are coming from."

"Stop. Please." I waved my right hand in the direction of the *Un-bridled*. "Contact the Reverend Fathers. I don't want to have to repeat everything. Especially, if I'm on the receiving end of another lecture."

Luc rested his hand on my ankle and did the heavy work of carrying me along with him into the link. For once, I appreciated his help. With the pain, shortness of breath, and exhaustion, I couldn't concentrate.

Anthea, what's wrong? Reverend Father Biming asked.

However, Luc couldn't block all of my discomfort from the link.

She summoned lightning during our first battle this morning, but the magic backlash from the skinwalkers threw her across the ship, and she broke a couple of ribs, Reverend Father, Shi Hua replied.

You can summon lightning? Shock poured from Reverend Father Jin.

Not always. And not with sufficient accuracy, I said dryly. *So please, don't ask me to teach anyone because I haven't discovered how or why I can do it.*

But you managed to destroy two enemy vessels, Yin Lin said.

I also managed to not set the Mars Tranquilus *on fire, too*, I snapped.

Perhaps we should focus on more pressing matters, Quan said. *Does Thief have any clue of where these langskips are coming from? Have any other nations in the eastern Old Continent been attacked?*

Both The Kingdom of Ryukyu and the United Dulohans have reported missing villages. Reverend Father Biming's worry trilled in our minds.

Missing villages? I asked. *Not just missing people from villages?*

In two remote fishing villages in Ryukyu, all the people were simply gone, Reverend Father Biming reported. *All the buildings, their belongings, and their equipment was there. Intact. No evidence of violence or blood.*

A similar situation happened with two Dulohans, Reverend Father Jin continued. *In this case, the home, workshops, and temples were gone as well.*

What do you mean by the structures were gone? Yin Li asked.

Exactly what I said, Reverend Father Jin said. *A trading fleet from one of the western Sea People kingdoms arrived at the first village to find only the foundations and the support poles. No people, no domesticated animals, no anything.*

A trading fleet from a neighboring dulohan found a second village in the same condition, Reverend Father Biming added. *Demon alarms rang in the third village. By the time the surrounding Dulohans responded, they found most of the villagers dead and fires raging out of control. The three priestesses of Mother herded the children to the tunnels that had been carved into the mountain south of the settlement.*

My stomach churned in a way that had nothing to do with the wine and pain powder. *When did these incidents happen?*

They all occurred two weeks before the attack on Chengzhou. Reverend Father Biming felt as nauseated as I did.

Now, we knew where the demons had come from. The renegades had used the innocent villagers to hatch demon eggs.

As you and Anthea feared. Shi Hua hugged herself, and Quan wrapped an arm around her shoulders.

I don't relish being correct, I said.

Neither do I. Bitterness raged through Reverend Father Biming. *However, the news becomes worse. Before we set sail to meet you, demon alarms sounded in the Xiongnu Confederation.*

They attempted to assassinate the Khan? Quan asked.

He's still alive, but his eldest son and a great number of his personal guard died defending him, Reverend Father Jin replied.

Have you sent aid to the Khan? Quan asked.

Yes, Your Highness. Reverend Father Feng is handling the repositioning of both Temple and civilian troops, Reverend Father Biming answered. *Your noble cousin is not happy, but he has no say when the empire responds to a request for help when there has been a demon attack.*

Are you saying none of our neighbors responded to the attack on Chengzhou? Doubt filled Quan's silent voice.

They all responded, Your Highness, Reverend Father Jin said. *Including Maurya.*

Thank you for coming to our rescue, I said. *We would not have survived the last five langskips without your assistance.*

Reverend Father Biming laughed. *And that is Chief Justice Anthea's gracious way of telling us we need to end the meeting before she rudely falls asleep on us.*

While part of your statement is true, old friend, everyone onboard the Mars Tranquilus *is grateful for your aid.* Quan sounded so sincere he surprised me. *Including me and my lady wife.*

We'll have a proper celebration when we reach Chengzhou, Your Highness, Lady Shi Hua, Reverend Father Biming said. *Have a good evening.*

I could barely keep my eyes open after Luc withdrew us from the link.

"Do you think I could pay the Assassins Guild to drop the price on Anthea's head and take care of my interfering cousin instead?" Quan said.

That question woke me up, and we all stared at him.

"I was joking," he said mildly.

"It might be worth asking about," I said. "Between them, the renegades, the demons and their ilk, eventually my luck will run out."

Chapter 30

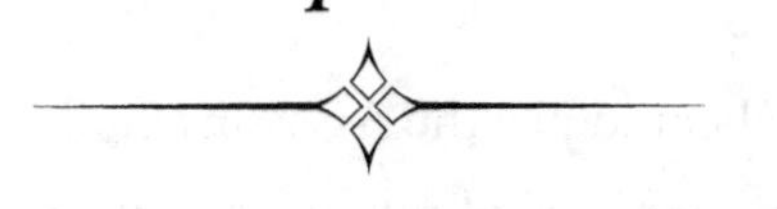

Despite the soma tears and my efforts to sleep through my pain, I found myself wide awake the next morning. I gritted my teeth against the ache of just moving my head. Luc, Yar, and Mateqai were gone.

"Do you need another soma tear, m'lady?" Jonata whispered.

"You can talk in a normal voice," Long Feather said. "I'm awake."

"I'm sorry if I woke you." I stared at the roof of our cabin. "I don't remember hurting this bad the last time I called lightning."

"That's because you didn't have demon magic blowback toss you halfway across the ship and break your ribs," Jonata said sourly. "Not to mention all the bruises."

"But I don't have bleeding from any bodily orifice, which means I should live." My chuckle turned into a groan at the ache in my chest.

"Serves you right for making such a poor jest." Jonata rolled out of the hammock she shared with Long Feather.

"May I have pain powder instead?" I asked. At Jonata's raised eyebrow, I amended my request, "I promise not to complain anymore."

She pursed her lips before she replied, "Yes, m'lady."

I didn't need to hear her thoughts to know she seriously considered slipping a soma tear into my wine anyway. It was a good thing I brought Jonata with me. Little Bear or Gina would have doctored my wine with the heavier drug without a second thought.

"Where is the Light contingent?" I asked.

"They were singing prayers at First Morning along with the Light clergy from the other three ships," Long Feather said. "I was surprised they didn't wake you." He rolled out of the hammock and aided me in sitting upright, using the pillows Yin Li left for me.

Jonata brought me a cup with the medicinal mixture.

I steeled myself and down the wine as fast as I could without choking. My action didn't avoid the bitter aftertaste. She took the cup from me and refilled it.

"I'll see about getting us some breakfast." Jonata sauntered out of the cabin in her sleeping tunic.

"Have we lost all decorum?" I asked sourly as I leaned against the pillows.

"No, m'lady," Long Feather said cheerfully as he changed his clothes. "We've been at sea for a month and a half and survived two battles with skinwalkers. And frankly, our uniforms could use a good cleaning."

"It's not only our uniforms." I sipped the plain wine. "I will pay for everyone onboard for a good soak in the baths."

"I won't let you forget, m'lady." Long Feather grinned.

The door opened, and Jonata returned with not only breakfast but Lady Shi Hua as well. My stomach rumbled at the sight of the bowls the women carried.

"The crews caught a few maguro this morning," the crown prince's wife said cheerfully.

It hurt to even raise my eyebrows. "Maguro?"

"It's the Fire Islands' name for the fish. It tastes similar to what you call thunnini."

I looked inside the bowl. "It's raw."

"Use this." Shi Hua held out the bottle she carried.

I frowned. "What is it?"

"Jiangyou. It kills any parasites and brings out the flavor in the fish."

"There's a reason humans don't eat raw meat," I muttered.

"Give me the jiangyou," Jonata insisted. Shi Hua handed over the bottle, and my warden poured the sauce over her raw fish and set the jar on the table. She picked up a morsel with her eating sticks and popped it into her mouth. My nose wrinkled at the acidic odor of the condiment.

Jonata swallowed. "Not bad."

"Let me try some," Long Father said. Jonata handed the jar to him, and he repeated the process. "A little on the salty side, but much better than jerky and hardtack. It's similar to the barley vinegar you prefer on fish, m'lady. You'll like it."

"Well, with that endorsement, I must try it," I said. I repeated my wardens' process and took a bite of the raw fish and sauce. I nodded as the flavor spread across my tongue. The sauce was richer than the vinegar I used, more savory. "This would be good on vegetables."

Shi Hua clapped her hands. "I can make you some of the dishes I grew up with when we reach Chengzhou."

"You mean instruct the palace cooks, m'lady," I said. "In a fortnight, you will be the empress of Jing."

Shi Hua's face fell and her back stiffened. "Wardens, may I speak with the chief justice alone?"

Long Feather and Jonata exchanged looks. "May we have the jiangyou?" he said.

"Take the damn sauce." I waved my left hand in a dismissive gesture, a little bothered by my wardens' priorities.

"We'll be right outside if you need us, Chief Justice," Jonata assured me.

Of that, I had no doubt. It wouldn't be the first time Long Feather eavesdropped on one of my private conversations. I didn't need this one to reach the fishwives though. I nodded, and the pair left the cabin, shutting the door behind them.

"Anthea—" She Hua started.

I held up my left index finger and quickly warded the room. A wave of dizziness hit me, and I nearly spilled the bowl of fish and sauce all over my bedding if Shi Hua hadn't caught it.

"I could have done that," Shi Hua said with a disgusted expression as she handed the bowl back to me.

"We need to talk, and the last thing I want is my wardens gossiping." I poked at the fish. "Shi Hua, I—"

"I'm sorry—" she said at the same time.

We both stopped and looked at each other.

"I'm so sorry I made you uncomfortable, Anthea." Her shoulders sagged, and she sat at the foot of the bed. "I didn't want either of us to die without telling you how I felt. In retrospect, it was stupid and unfair of me to do so. I'm a married woman now, and you love the high brother, and you've both been through so much because of the war and the edict—" She burst into tears.

"Oh, Shi Hua, I never wanted to break your heart." My own eyes burned. "You're the closest thing I ever had to a sister. If I had any inkling about your feelings, I-I would have let you down gently before now."

"And maybe I should have said something before I married Po." She swiped her cheeks with the sleeves of her tunic. "My feelings for you are not fair to him either."

"So why didn't you say something when the edict came down?"

An odd expression crossed her face. "I don't think you and I were what the Reverend Mothers and Fathers had in mind when they issued the breeding edict."

"Logically, though, that's when you should have approached me," I said dryly. "Not the day after I officiated your wedding."

She giggled despite the yellow tears running down her face. "That was rather idiotic on my part, wasn't it?"

"A little bit." I took another bite of fish. "I apologize. This is really much better than I thought it would be."

"Then I'll instruct the palace chefs to make sure you have plenty of jiangyou while you are in residence as our guest." She sniffed and smiled at the same time.

"I would enjoy that very much, Your Majesty." I smiled in return. "Can I still count you as a friend?"

"No." Her smile widened. "But you can count me as a sister."

Chapter 31

A week later, the *Mars Tranquilus* and the Jing ships sailed around the southern end of Ryukyu Island to their main port of Naha on the western side. Of course, my knowledge of our route was based on reports from Shi Hua and my wardens. Captain Titus, his first officer Iniki, and his second Officer Little Squirrel were all rather adamant I stay in my cabin for the last seven days of our voyage.

Apparently, they were all worried I would do something foolish, like fall overboard.

Shi Hua and Yin Li made a point of entertaining me while I lay trapped in my cabin. At least, they didn't object to me pacing the deck in order to exercise like Luc and the wardens did every time they caught me out of bed. My ribs were broken, not my leg bones.

Neither would anyone let me leave the ship until Reverend Father Biming brought a healer back to the *Mars Tranquilus* for me once we had docked. Normally, I would fight a healing tooth and nail. I hated how exhausted and out of sorts I felt afterward, but not being able to take a deep breath now was driving me insane.

Well, more insane than I already was.

Of course, the Ryukyuan healer and his apprentice couldn't decide if they were more fascinated in meeting a foreign justice or by my red eyes. Apparently, justices rarely left their Temples in this part of the world.

Since I was the only sighted justice ever recorded, they asked all sorts of questions that had absolutely nothing to do with my cracked ribs. The Reverend Father must have sensed my irritation despite the fact he was a quicksilver. He insisted they drop the questions until after the healing.

The healer was slightly embarrassed for not making my welfare his top priority. His apprentice's curiosity outweighed his chagrin.

I could breathe easier when the healing was complete, but as I expected, I was bone-tired considering the amount of damage to my body. I fell asleep while the apprentice cared for his master with his own post-healing exhaustion.

When I woke the next morning, Jonata and I headed to Naha's public baths near the Temple District. While I was being healed and sleeping off the magic hangover, my wonderful wardens had delivered both my uniforms and theirs to a local washerwoman Reverend Father Biming had recommended. The rest of the passengers had spent yesterday afternoon getting cleaned, plucked, and otherwise groomed prior to our arrival in Jing.

Thankfully, everyone we encountered spoke the Peaceful Sea trade tongue. I paid the gold for Jonata and me to have a private bathing room. The Ryukyu public baths put the Issuran ones to shame. The pool itself was formed from a single piece of carved basalt. Water came in through fired clay pipes, heated by the steam and melted rock beneath their islands. Their soaps and oils held delightful scents, including some very expensive jasmine. It gave me another idea for gifts for everyone back home.

"This is glorious." I leaned my back against the side of the huge stone tub and scrubbed the layer of filth from the bottom of my left foot with a pumice stone. "Part of me wants to soak in this pool for a month."

Jonata laughed. Her skin was nearly as red as our bathing water. "Certain officials are not happy we're staying here for as long as we are."

"They'd better understand the necessity," I grumbled. "It will take more than a candlemark to put together the lady's trousseau."

As much as I hated to leave, neither of us dawdled at the baths. However, it was wonderful to feel clean again. But as we walked back to the harbor under the spring sun, Jonata clasped her hand in mine and guided me toward the market, ostensibly to purchase some gifts for her family back in Issura.

Silently, she said, *We are being followed, m'lady.*

The two women dressed as Fire Islands merchants who followed us from the harbor?

Must you always keep information to yourself in order to appear omniscient? Jonata grumbled.

I laughed. *I'm used to keeping Little Bear and Gina on their toes.*

You mean annoy them as much as they annoy you, Jonata said. *May I point out that neither Long Feather nor I endeavor to annoy you?*

A shop keeper offered us sample of a dried fruit she called kaki. It had mild taste and wasn't too sweet, an altogether delightful pome. I purchased a small pouch from her.

I apologize, Warden, I said as we continued through the market. *I wasn't trying to do that with you. As a hunted animal, I've become very aware of my surroundings.*

They could be Assassins Guild. Jonata casually glanced around at some trinkets in order to keep an eye on the pair following us. *I need to get you back to the ship.*

If they wanted us dead, they could have poisoned our bath water, I noted.

Let's not give them any suggestions, Jonata replied dryly. She finished bargaining with the jeweler and tucked the jade earrings she purchased for her mother in her belt pouch.

What if we question them? I suggested.

You don't have jurisdiction to truthspell them in Ryukyu, m'lady.

Who said anything about truthspelling them? I grinned.

Jonata shook her head. *If I end up in the local gaol, you* will *pay my fines.*

The women who followed us were good. A couple of times, I believed we had lost them, only for them to reappear a block or two later.

Finally, Jonata and I darted in front of a pair of oxen pulling a large wagon full of manure. The animal's driver yelled at us, but we were already racing down an alley. We took a left on a main street, and then another left down an even narrower alley. We ducked into a deep doorway and waited.

We didn't have too long to wait. I may not speak the Fire Islands language, but I recognized it when others spoke it. Sandals slapped against the sandstone pavers, coming closer and closer.

Now! We rushed our stalkers.

I used the fighting techniques Shi Hua had taught me, and my target landed hard on her back. I dug my left boot heel into her right wrist and rested the edge of my sword against her throat.

Jonata didn't have as much luck. The second woman tore free of my warden's grasp. However, our second stalker didn't run. Jonata danced a few steps back to draw her sword and block the second stalker's exit.

"Forgive our clumsiness, Chief Justice." The second woman straightened and held up her hands in surrender. "We were ordered to protect you, but not interfere with your visit to Naha."

"By who?" I demanded.

"By the Reverend Father of Thief of the Kingdom of Ryukyu."

Chapter 32

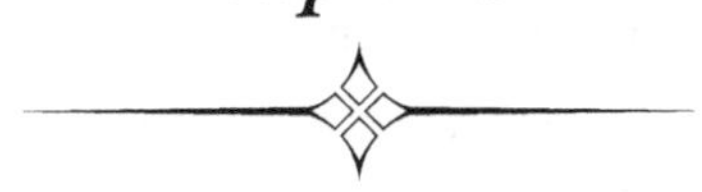

I frowned. "And you have proof of this claim?"

The second woman looked at her partner, still lying on the sandstone pavers lining the alley.

"Show her," the woman with my sword at her throat said.

"I'm going to retrieve a coin from my right pocket." The second woman moved very slowly and reached into the said pocket. The coin she produced was nickel. I examined it magically as well. No spells were hidden in the metal.

"Hand it to my warden," I ordered.

She reached out as far toward Jonata as she could while keeping her eyes locked on mine. Jonata caught the coin when the second woman dropped it.

"It's similar to the Assassins Guild coins," Jonata reported in Diné. "But nickel instead of pewter. The symbol for the Temple of Thief is stamped on one side, but it's not scratched through. I don't recognize the symbol on the other side, but it's the picture writing many nations use on this side of the Peaceful Sea."

I spoke in the trade tongue. "Then it's a good thing we know someone who can verify their information." I smiled at the woman under my boot and sword. "Well, you were smart enough to allow me to eat and bathe this morning, so I won't kill you yet. However, you and your partner are coming with us to the docks. If you even think about escaping or harming my warden, I'll have fish bait for the remainder of our journey."

Both women were smart enough to remain silent and cooperate as we walked back to the *Unbridled*.

When we reached the berth where the *Unbridled* was docked, I called out for Hadar without using his Temple title. As far as I would let these women know, he was simply the *Unbridled*'s first officer.

His orange-bright face peered over the railing. "In trouble already, Chief Justice? We only docked yesterday."

"I'm well aware of that," I shouted back. "I need to speak with your captain. Now."

"He's in negotiations with a merchant at the moment, m'lady," Hadar said.

"Now. Or I'll board your ship and take my very bad mood out on you," I shouted while jabbing my left forefinger at the ramp.

Hadar shook his head. "Very well. One moment." He disappeared from the railing.

I tapped the toe of my boot on the dock boards. Jonata waited calmly between our stalkers and the shore. The two women dressed as merchants quivered, and their skin color brightened a bit. However, I wasn't sure whether it was an act or if they were truly nervous.

They couldn't possibly know the identity of the captain of the *Un-bridled*. So, why would the Ryukyu Reverend Father of Thief send two of his people to follow me around Naha? I sighed. Unless they were telling the truth. And the only reason they knew my identity was due to the nasty little adherent of Thief currently hiding in his cabin.

Hadar appeared at the railing. "The captain will see you now, Chief Justice."

I stomped up the ship's ramp. Yes, the women's footsteps behind me were a little too quiet and a little too sure. While Shi Hua had technically been Light, she'd also trained with Conflict and Thief in preparation for her position as Quan's personal bodyguard. I'd been around her and all of Orrin's Thief contingent for nearly two full years. I wasn't sure what I was angrier about—that I didn't recognize the pair as Thief priestesses or that Biming believed I couldn't take care of myself.

Hadar led us to the captain's cabin. He knocked, opened the door, and said, "Chief Justice Anthea of Orrin, Duchy in the queendom of Issura, to see you, sir."

I strode into the cabin. Another man sat with Biming. He was dressed as a Ryukyuan merchant, but his clothing was as artificial as the women who had been stalking me and Jonata all morning.

"Are you two deliberately trying to get me beheaded for the crime of killing fellow clergy for being idiots?" I wasn't shouting. No, I sounded more like High Brother Jax in his wolf form.

Biming looked at the other man and said something in Ryukyuan.

The so-called merchant rose and bowed to me before he spoke in the trade tongue. "No offense was meant, Chief Justice. Even here, we know about the Assassins Guild's price on both yours and the Lady Shi Hua's heads."

I glanced at the two women, or rather Thief priestesses. No wonder they were nervous. They'd royally embarrassed the head of their Temple. I turned back to Biming and his friend.

"I don't like telling anyone, and most definitely not a Reverend Father or a Reverend Mother, how to conduct their affairs, but these two need some additional training. Their behavior needs to match their dress."

Biming said something in a teasing manner to the Ryukyuan Reverend Father of Thief in the local language. I didn't need a translation for the other priest's response. The curt syllable was obviously an insult.

"You two can ridicule each other at a later date," I snapped.

"W-we apologize profusely, Lady Justice," the woman I'd held at sword point murmured. "When we were told you were a priestess of Balance with sight, we did not take the information seriously. Such things are simply not done in this part of the world."

I pushed back my hood so the two women could see my eyes. They both gasped at their first good look at my face.

My point was made, but knowing Biming, he would merely ask his Ryukyuan counterpart to assign someone else. Someone whose loyalties may be superseded by the obscene amount of gold the Assassins Guild offered for my head.

"If you truly regret the irritation you have caused, then I ask two favors."

"Of course, Lady Justice," the second woman replied.

"First, I ask you both to submit to my truthspell so I may be assured of your integrity." I sighed. "Second, can you recommend any dressmakers who could outfit a lady of Jing royalty with very short notice?"

The second woman glanced at her Reverend Father. "Your second service would require a hefty fee. Are you asking us to pay it?"

"Certainly not." I smiled. "I merely want to ensure my little sister is appropriately attired now that she's married to a member of the Jing imperial family. Unfortunately, we were forced to leave Issura before I could make proper arrangements."

Both women bowed, and the first one said, "We would be honored to assist your sister in acquiring her trousseau, Lady Justice."

Chapter 33

Biming finally made formal introductions. "Reverend Father Ogusuku of Thief, may I present Chief Justice Anthea of Balance?"

He inclined his head. In turn, I executed a formal bow. "My apologies for interrupting your meeting, Reverend Fathers."

Reverend Father Ogusuku snorted. "A lie is a poor way to start an acquaintance, Chief Justice."

"My sentiment would be far more sincere if your counterpart from Jing hadn't approached you for assistance behind my back." I glared at Biming. "Assistance which was unnecessary."

He shot me an expression of faux innocence. "But you just said you needed aid in finding a dressmaker for the Lady Shi Hua's trousseau."

"Don't, Reverend Father." I slashed my hand through the air. "Just don't."

Reverend Father Ogusuku introduced his two priestesses as Jade and Jasmine. I knew those weren't their real names, but I also understood the reasoning for giving me false names given their order's roles and responsibilities.

The two women quietly submitted to my truthspell and even more surprisingly didn't try to fight it. I did nothing further to shame them during my questioning. It wasn't their fault their Reverend Father didn't fully prepare them for dealing with me.

Before we left the cabin, I glared at Biming. "You and I are not finished, but our conversation will need to wait."

Reverend Father Ogusuku scowled at me. "Do you speak to your own Reverend Mother with such disrespect?"

Biming slapped the table and roared with laughter. "This is nothing compared to how she treats Reverend Mother Alara of Issura."

"Reverend Father, I have no wish to make an enemy of you." I paused to choose my next words carefully. "However, my queen has given me a specific task, my Reverend Mother agreed to allow me to serve Queen Teodora, and I will complete that task regardless of who may try to stop me. This task is no danger to you, your king, or the people of Ryukyu. I would not have accepted the responsibility of this task if it brought harm to innocent nations or people."

"Innocence can be subjective, Chief Justice." His wry smile reminded me of High Brother Talbert. For some strange reason, a twinge of homesickness ran through me.

"My criteria is simple, Reverend Father. Are you trying to kill me or another person without the benefit of a trial?"

The Ryukyuan priest inclined his head. "Forgive me for questioning your principles."

"There is no need for forgiveness where no offense was taken." I inclined my own head in return. We left the *Unbridled* to collect the rest of our party for my next mission.

The sisters who owned the shop Jade and Jasmine recommended kept asking me what I thought about fabrics, and worse, the colors. Not because the seamstresses learned I was a justice with sight, but because I was the one with the gold.

I deferred to Yin Li who actually had a clue about what Shi Hua would need as the wife of the Jing emperor. Even Jonata and Mateqai were able to pitch suggestions. Long Feather looked as bored as I felt, and he did his best to watch out for my safety without getting in the way.

My assistance finally came in when Shi Hua needed places to hide weapons within her new outfits. The seamstresses didn't even blink at my ideas. I had a feeling they did a great deal of work for the local Temple of Thief, much like the silversmith Govind and his business partner back in Orrin created specialty items for both Balance and Thief.

The seamstresses promised Shi Hua's trousseau in three days. I wondered if they were being a little overenthusiastic in their estimate, but Jade assured me the project would be completed when they said it would be.

The air was much cooler when we stepped outside, but there was no orb above the city skyline or the surrounding mountains. As soon as the thought flitted through my head, the Temple bells started ringing First Evening.

I turned to Jade and Jasmine. "I would be honored if you ladies would join us for the evening meal."

Jasmine bowed. "Please allow us the honor of providing the evening meal, m'lady. It is our way of apologizing for disturbing your visit to our kingdom."

I grinned. "I think you more than compensated me by not overcharging me for Lady Shi Hua's trousseau."

Jasmine exchanged a look with Jade, and I had no doubt they were silently discussing plans for the night. "In Ryukyu, it is customary for the bride's friends to take her to Mother to pray for a fruitful marriage and healthy children. May we worship with you before we take our evening meal?"

Maybe I was overly trusting, but I had a feeling I knew what they planned. I inclined my head. "We would be honored."

Jasmine and Jade led the way to Naha's Temple District. Paper lamps powered by Knowledge magic hung from poles along the street.

"Why don't you use Light magic lamps?" I asked.

"Because Light magic illumination needs glass or alabaster to contain the spell without a priest or priestess present," Jade said. "With our frequent ground quakes, broken shards are far more dangerous than torn paper."

"And given that demon armies are on the move again, it would be a waste of Light talent," Jasmine added.

Their words made me question why our own Temple of Knowledge back in Orrin didn't provide public light in the evenings. Such illumination would cut down on petty theft and pickpockets, especially around the docks and warehouses. Not to mention, Issura occasionally had its own issues with ground quakes. If we could replace the oil lamps on the streets, it would be safer for everyone.

High Sister Mariana would throw a tantrum over extra duties for her Temple. But the idea merited some thought since it would assist in preventing crime and provide illumination during our constant crises. I would have to present the idea to Duke Marco, Magistrate DiCook, and the city council when we returned. They might have an easier time prodding Mariana into action.

Of course, that was assuming she still held the Knowledge seat in Orrin when we got home. Though I had verbally reprimanded her, every other Temple seat but Luc had filed a formal complaint against her with the Issuran home Temple of Knowledge after she failed to respond to a demon alarm last summer. Not only had she failed to respond, she forbade her clergy and wardens to respond as well. In fact, Issura's Reverend Father of Knowledge had sent me a private letter asking why I hadn't filed a complaint.

The Temples in Ryukyu resembled noble estates rather than places of worship. Wide moats of flowing water surrounded each of the twelve demesnes. Wooden bridges connected the main thoroughfare to the Temples. Gardens and flowerbeds filled the yard between the bridge and each Temple's main entrance. A wide path with stone pavers led to the Temple steps while gravel side trails meandered through the riot of plants.

No, the demesnes weren't like nobles estates. They were more like the twin manses and gardens of the Healers Guilds with the same peaceful air. However, they were as huge as the Issuran home Temples in Standora. Each one took up two city blocks.

My party followed the two Ryukyuan women over the bridge and up the path of the Temple of Mother. Stone steps led up to the main doors. The first floor walls were also stone, but wood finished the second story. Even the four corner towers followed the same building style.

The two wardens at the doors nodded acknowledgement to me and the Issuran wardens since we were the only ones in Temple uniforms. Otherwise, they simply watched the traffic and visitors with keen attention.

The Ryukyuan wardens dressed slightly differently than those of Issura. Steel thread wove through the silk coats and pants they wore. They carried two swords in their wide sashes, one longer than the other. Both blades were single-edged and curved. However, like my own wardens, I suspected they carried other weapons hidden upon their person. All Ryukyuan wardens I'd seen so far, regardless of their gender, wore their hair wrapped in a knot at the crown and held in place by a silver hairpin. Considering the damage the Love priestesses back home could do with a simple hairpin, I shouldn't underestimate the Ryukuans.

The interior of the sanctuary was similar to the order of Mother in Issura and alien at the same time. More paper lanterns powered by Knowledge magic filled the space. The statue of Mother consisted of a single piece of carved jade dressed in the simple silk dress of a Ryukyuan common woman.

A priestess spoke with Jade before she led us before the statue. Jasmine motioned for us to sit on the center bench while Jade escorted Shi Hua to the altar. Mateqai moved to follow her, but Jasmine grabbed his elbow.

"You are not her husband," she murmured.

Mateqai shot a pleading look toward me. I couldn't blame him. He was loyal to a fault when it came to Shi Hua's safety.

"Jasmine, Mateqai's clan considers the lady as his sister." I also kept my voice low. "It's not uncommon for a brother to accompany a noble woman in Issura when her husband is not available."

Jasmine repeated our request to the mother at the altar. She murmured a few words in the Ryukyuan language. Jasmine nodded. "It is allowed."

Mateqai joined Shi Hua with the mother. While the language was foreign, the ritual itself was not. I prayed silently that Mother would watch out for Shi Hua in her new role in life.

When the blessing was done, I approached the mother and pressed a gold coin into her palm. "Thank you on behalf of my sister," I said in the trade tongue.

The priestess laughed and shook her head as she placed the coin back in my hand. "Here, there is no donation between sisters." She used the word that could mean priestess or sibling. "I hope our sister finds satisfaction outside of Temple life."

"I hope so, too, Mother."

Instead of escorting us back to the main boulevard, Jade and Jasmine led our little group through the side hallway toward the priestesses' private quarters. Jade knocked on a door, which was opened by a female warden of Mother.

The warden scowled at us, and I had the impression Jade was having to do some type of negotiation. Finally, the warden let us enter.

Inside the room, two mothers worked on embroidery while a second male warden stood guard near the far wall. The only furniture was the two chairs the mothers used. However, lanterns of various types hung on hooks along two of the walls. One of the priestesses rose from her seat and approached. She greeted Jade warmly in the Ryukyuan language before she turned to me.

"Greetings, Chief Justice." Thankfully, she used the trade tongue.

"And greetings to you, Mother." I inclined my head.

The priestess crossed to the wall where the male warden stood. She whispered a spell. Magic caressed my skin as the stone folded back on itself.

"You are still using your tunnel system?"

"Ours terminate at the Sea of Flames." Jasmine grinned. "The demons would have to learn how to swim first to access our system."

"They can climb across the ceiling of the sea cave," I replied.

"They can try." Jasmine reached for an oil lamp.

"Save your resources." Shi Hua flicked her fingers and a Light ball formed just above her palm. I couldn't see it, but I could definitely feel it. "I need to stay in practice on something besides killing demons."

Jasmine inclined her head. "As you wish, m'lady."

The mother gathered two glass balls hanging from the walls inside which Shi Hua could place her spells. I passed one to Jonata, and Jade carried the second one. Jasmine bent over and entered the passage. Shi Hua and the light ball she held went next, followed immediately by Mateqai.

I ducked through the opening and followed the trio to a narrow landing. Shi Hua's light ball showed a carved set of stone stairs leading downward. They were hand-chiseled, much like the Balance gaol's spiral staircase back home.

When I reached the main tunnel, the structure abruptly changed. There were no cut marks on the walls. The formation almost looked like wax that had been melted and dripped before it solidified. Furthermore, the walls didn't glow pale lavender from creatures too tiny to see like the tunnels and caves back home. Something else lived on these walls. The patches of creatures glowed gold, and the walls themselves were a brilliant green. I reached out and brushed my fingers along a patch of the wall without any beings. The wall was warm to my touch.

"Is something wrong, Chief Justice?" Jonata asked.

"I know the Ryukyuans use their hot springs to heat bathing water." I chuckled. "I didn't consider those same springs would heat the surrounding rock." I turned to Jasmine. "You would flood the tunnels with the boiling water from the hot springs if demons manage to breach the sea entrances, wouldn't you?"

"Excellent observation, Chief Justice." Jasmine laughed. "It also helps that several of the springs contain acid. According to the histories, the boiling acid and water made the demons think twice about crawling into our tunnels from the sea exits."

"Fascinating," I murmured. "Is the acid the reason for the strange drip marks?"

"No, m'lady. This was an ancient lava tube." Jasmine continued walking. "Molten rock flows like melted fat." She pointed at the sharp stalactites overhead. "Sometimes, the top layer solidifies while the lava below it continues to ooze toward the sea. Eventually, the reservoir of melted rock is exhausted, leaving empty chambers and tubes through the cooled stone. They saved the Temples a great deal of time and effort in Ryukyu."

I laughed. "Considering Orrin's Balance gaol alone had to be hand-carved out of the bedrock, your Temples were very fortunate."

"The Twelve grant us that small gift in the face of typhoons, tsunamis, and ground quakes." Jasmine smirked.

We walked much farther than I ever had in the Orrin tunnel system, but then, the Naha Temples were so much larger. I was rather glad I'd given in to the healing, and I had a day to sleep it off. Otherwise, I would never had made it to the side tunnel Jasmine guided us down.

The cat's paw touch of Thief magic glided over my skin as she touched a section of the wall and whispered her spell. I should have known we would end up here at some point during our visit. Biming was here after all.

And that man knew how to get his way no matter what anyone else thought.

The last time resulted in the loss of the city of Tandor. What would be the price I would pay this time?

Chapter 34

When I stepped into the Ryukyu Temple of Thief, I noticed they had the same security situation as Mother had. Except the two priests had a table and played chess rather than embroider.

The warden by the entrance sheathed his swords. "Welcome, Chief Justice."

"Thank you for not stabbing me." I smiled. "It's a relief that one Temple of Thief waits to hear who's entering their building before jabbing their swords in my direction."

"If we had the number of demon incidents you've had in Issura, I'm sure I would be much more stabby." He grinned.

"Quit flirting with the chief justice, Warden Tamashiro," one of the priests snapped. "She is a guest of the Reverend Father."

The warden ignored his superior. "Perhaps you would care to tour Naha tomorrow, m'lady. The public gardens are the finest on any of the islands."

"Taking the breeding edict a little too seriously, Warden?" Two could play this game.

"I do have passive Light talent as well as a token active thief talent. I'm sure I could provide whatever you need while you visit our beautiful islands."

"Aren't you going to do something?" Mateqai hissed to Jonata in Issuran.

"If his token Thief talent is anything like the ambassador's, it won't work on the chief justice," she responded in kind.

"Is the heir to Jing's talent the ability to charm anyone into his bed?" the second Thief priest asked in our language.

That drew a sharp bark of laughter from both of my own wardens.

"It is," Jonata replied. "The only reason the chief justice hasn't stabbed the prince is her respect for the rule of law and our queen. However, if Warden Tamashiro wishes to try his luck, who am I to stop him?"

She turned back to the Tamashiro and switched to the Peaceful Sea tongue. "Warden, it's not just my lady's sword skills that earned her the nickname the Red Justice."

I took her statement as my cue and pushed back my hood. "Surely, Jonata, the good warden is open-minded about who he takes to his bed."

Tamashiro's throat knot bobbed, but I credited him for maintaining his flirtatious expression. "Balance Herself deemed variety an excellent quality when She created the universe."

"This is true." I smiled. "So what makes you different than any other man? I had to drug Huizhong, one of the crown prince's guards to make him lay still in my cabin."

Tamashiro's mouth fell open while the ladies and the two priests laughed.

I turned to the priest who had spoken Issuran. "I assume Lady Shi Hua, myself, and our party are supposed to dine with Reverend Fathers Ogusuku and Biming this evening."

The Thief priest nodded. "Yes, my lady."

"This way, Chief Justice." Jasmine gestured toward the conventional door in the room.

I followed her while the stone grinded as it folded itself closed behind us.

◆

When we reached Reverend Father Ogusuku's formal dining room, we discovered the crown prince and Luc had arrived with Biming. Dishes were brought in by the Temple staff. Jade was kind enough to explain each one. Ryukyu already had spring vegetables available since they're climate was much warmer than Issura's. The conversation remained light and pleasant until the final course was served.

I'd taken my first bite of what Jade called sama andagi when Reverend Father Ogusuku said, "Our king invites the crown prince of Jing and his entourage to dine with him at the Crimson Palace tomorrow evening."

I swallowed the sweet fried dough, the taste no longer as delightful as it had been a moment before. "Why didn't he send an official messenger to us at the docks?'

"The same reason I didn't send a formal notice to him I was here." Quan clicked his tongue. "Really, Anthea. For such a brilliant woman, you can be quite obtuse at times."

At Reverend Father Ogusuku's shocked look and Biming's snicker, I shrugged. "You'll have to excuse the prince. He's still rather irritated I refused his offers for bedplay prior to his marriage."

"And after his marriage?" Jade teased.

I smiled. "I've seen his lady wife in action against demons. I would be a fool to give her a reason to kill me."

"I'd only stab you for bedding him over me," Shi Hua shot back.

Everyone laughed except Quan, who made a face.

"Now, I know what to expect when we reach Chengzhou," he muttered.

"You have to admit, Your Highness, this is Balance's way of evening Her scales for your past amorous adventures." Biming grinned.

"I don't recall you complaining," Quan responded.

"Is this dinner a good idea?" I turned to Reverend Father Ogusuku. "I mean no disrespect to you or your king, but I'm under orders from both Queen Teodora and Reverend Mother Alara to get Prince Po home alive."

"You believe my order or my king would assassinate the heir to the Jing throne?"

Would you like me to find you some dog feces to smear through the Temple while you're at it? Luc whispered in my mind.

I ignored him. "No, Reverend Father. I fear the demons and their renegade allies would take advantage of your king's hospitality to kill him and Crown Prince Po in one strike."

Reverend Father Ogusuku inclined his head. "And that was the exact same advice I presented to His Majesty. However, he believes good relations with the new ruler of a neighboring nation takes priority over our fears for their safety. He offers the use of three squads of soldiers in addition to the forces of Jing and Issura at Crown Prince Po's disposal. Surely, the best of three different countries can protect him."

I looked at Quan. "The choice is yours, Your Highness."

His right eyebrow rose. There was so much loaded in that gesture, chief of which was his unspoken question, "Are you really letting me decide?"

He turned back to Reverend Father Ogusuku. "My party and I would be delighted to join King Sho Kinpuku for dinner."

Chapter 35

As promised, three squads of Ryukyuan soldiers arrived at Third Afternoon to escort us to the Crimson Palace. However, the soldiers carried shields and their swords were of medium length with a one-handed grip. In addition, clergy and their wardens who had been invited to the dinner accompanied the soldiers, including three justices.

The chief justice from the metallic thread embroidered on her robes had her warden lead her to me. She bowed.

"I am Chief Justice Fumiko. Please forgive the absence of our Reverend Mother. She has become quite frail as her age advances."

"A pleasure, Chief Justice." Silently, I added, *Or does she find state functions as tedious as my own Reverend Mother does?*

Fumiko chuckled. *Actually, my Reverend Mother enjoys these occasions far more than I do.*

Then you and I will get along fine. Aloud, I said, "Please extend my apologies to your Reverend Mother for not calling on her sooner. May I do so tomorrow?"

"Of course, Chief Justice." She inclined her head.

"Please call me Anthea," I said. "Otherwise, the constant titles make it sound like I'm talking to myself."

Our procession set off across the city. Citizens stared and murmured, but for once, there was no pointing and ugly comments about the Red Justice.

At least, I didn't think there were ugly comments because no one was pointing at me and whispering in any language.

Luc watched while Anthea spoke and laughed with the Ryukyuan chief justice. His heart warmed at seeing her interacting with her counterparts. Maybe that was what she needed even more than High Sister Mya's help. Reverend Mother Alara had caused Anthea nearly as much heartache as her birth mother had.

The procession passed the Ryukyuan version of Government House. In their case though, the bureaucracy was spread out in a series of three low building on each side of the thoroughfare. They entered the square between the bureaucratic offices and the royal residence when the Temple bells tolled the demon alarm code. Weapons were instantly drawn.

Ahead of them, the gates of the Crimson Palace slammed shut. It was the wise move for the palace guards to protect their king, but it left Crown Prince Quan and his escorts in the open pavilion with no defensible place to retreat.

"Shi Hua, get the prince to the palace!" The order popped out of his mouth before he could stop it.

However, she didn't argue. Both she and her aunt Yin Li grabbed Quan and dragged him in the direction of the service door of the guardhouse. Mateqai raced after them.

Only for the drawbridge over the first moat to rise, cutting the prince off from any hope of shelter.

Screams rose from the rear of the procession. Luc turned to Yar. His warden held Yin Li's son on his hip.

"Orders, High Brother?"

"Get me and Yin Shang up on the first wall of the palace!"

Luc swung on his crutches after the warden. Yar hoisted up Yin Shang and then Luc.

He straddled the wall and strung his bow. The switch from sword to bow had been a pain in his back side, but with his left foot gone, thanks to the renegades, he couldn't maneuver on his crutches and swing a blade at the same time.

"What can I do, High Brother?" Yin Li asked with an earnest look on his face.

"Pray to the Twelve we can end this quickly, good sir."

Demons surged through the ranks of the procession. Luc chose his targets carefully. He couldn't afford to be distracted by the carnage. As soldiers died, Brother Jian, one of the young Jing priests of Light, would grab the arrows from the fallen's quivers. Half he ordered Yar to deliver to Luc. The other half he used to cover Anthea.

Of course, Luc's heart was in the middle of the battle. She must have been silently speaking with her fellow justices. The Ryukyuan priestesses were using some of her tricks with time, which allowed Reverend Father Jin and the Light contingents to gain the upper hand.

Luc almost breathed in relief until Anthea chased after a demon in the direction of the public gardens. When a human stepped from behind a tree, bile rose in his throat at the taint of demon magic coming from the man.

A skinwalker.

Then the world turned itself inside out. A tear in the fabric of space and time like the stunt their attackers had pulled in the middle of the Peaceful Sea in the direction the demon and Anthea ran. She screamed an order, and Brother Jian shot the skinwalker. She lunged for the demon as it stepped through the rip in reality.

Only to plunge through the rift herself and disappear.

"ANTHEA!"

191

To learn what happens to Anthea after she falls into the demon hole, turn the page for a preview of *Invasion!*

Invasion

The Crimson Palace, the Kingdom of Ryukyu, Year of the Twelve 1979

Anthea, Chief Justice of the city of Orrin from the Queendom of Issura, ducked the slashing black talons of the demon who rushed her. Sweat stung her eyes as she whispered words of her spell, charging her sword with Balance magic. Her backswing sliced into the demon's neck.

Its screech of fury and pain blended with the shouts and screams of the soldiers, wardens, and clergy around her as they engaged the demon army. Issuran, Jing, and Ryukyu languages mixed in a cacophony punctuated by the chittering tongue of the demons. The alien scent of their foes mixed with the coppery odor of human blood and the stink of the loosened bowels of the dead.

An arrow charged with Light magic whizzed by her head. The second demon wailed, a sound reminiscent of fingernails on slate. Both the demon and the arrow collapsed into a pile of ash.

Despite the first demon's efforts to increase its body density to trap her weapon, Anthea wrenched her sword free from its neck. Brother Jian of the Jing Empire's Temple of Light launched another arrow into the third demon. Anthea charged her sword with magic once again as she danced backward from her own foe.

The demon's swing to disembowel her was slow and clumsy from the effects of her first spell. Since all demons were the darkest shade of black to her, its loss of coordination and lack of its normal speed was the only indication the demon was aging faster than normal.

Anthea thrust her sword into what passed for the demon's chest. Her foe crumpled to dust as her spell discharged through it. Despite their much longer lifespans, not even the demons could escape the ravages of time. And time was the domain of the Temple of Balance.

She panted and looked around her. Her heart tried to force its way up her throat. Ambassador Quan of Jing along with his wife Shi Hua and Sister Yin Li of the Temple of Love, had been backed against the abutment of the first bridge into the Crimson Palace.

Not Ambassador Quan any longer. He was now Crown Prince Bao Quan Po of the Jing Empire. If the Issuran and Jing escorts didn't keep him alive and get him home to be crowned emperor, Jing would fall into a civil war.

Then the demons would eat the leftovers.

The Ryukyu guards didn't dare open the gates to the palace. Not even to save their own forces. Despite the palace's multiple gates and intricate moat system, the demons would overrun the palace guards in a matter of heartbeats. It rested on the clergy and their wardens to reinforce the soldiers and keep the demons' attention away from the evacuating civilians.

"Jonata!"

Her warden lit the flashbang in her hand and tossed it in the middle of a group of demons harassing High Brother Luc of Light and Yin Li's young son Yin Shang where they perched on the outer moat wall. The flashbang exploded. Luc used the demons' disorientation to fire Light-charged arrows at them. Within three heartbeats, the demons crumbled into dust.

"With me!" Anthea shouted. Where in Light was Warden Mateqai? He wouldn't leave Shi Hua's side unless—

She shoved the ugly thought away. Now was not the time. Not when they needed to deal with the demons first or more people would die.

Jonata drew her sword and the long knife she used for defense and raced after Anthea. Together, they killed two of the demons at the back of the pack threatening Quan, Shi Hua, and Yin Li.

The pack split, and the back half whirled and charged the two Issuran women. Anthea threw up a quick ward. She rocked back on her heels from the increased mass of the half dozen of their enemies slamming into her magical shield.

"Drop your ward, Justice!" Brother Jin yelled from behind her.

Anthea released her ward while she and Jonata backpedaled. More arrows charged with Light magic flew between them. Four of the demons crumbled into dust. Brother Fa of Wildling, in his second form of a gigantic feline called a tiger, ripped off the head of the fifth demon.

The sixth demon galloped on all fours toward the City of Naha's public gardens. Anthea raced after it. More sweat dripped into her eyes. She needed to kill it. Sundown was moments away, and then her fellow clergy would be at a huge disadvantage.

Ahead, a figure stepped from behind a flowering tree. The greenish-gray skin gave away its identity as much as the demon magic it wielded.

Skinwalker. A human sorcerer who studied and apprenticed to the enemies of the human race. Using demon magic corrupted the person until they were no longer human.

It flung a spell at Anthea. She threw up a ward, but the impact knocked her on her arse.

The skinwalker cast a second spell. Anthea gasped at the explosion of colors. It was quite literally a rip in reality. Bile surged up her throat. The demon raced for the tear. She forced herself to her feet.

"What in Light's name!"

"Jian! Take out the skinwalker!" she ordered as she raced the demon to the portal.

Light magic surged behind her. A shrill scream filled the air.

The rip flickered. Anthea lunged for the demon.

And found herself flailing in midair. No demon. No ground. No sky.

Then she fell.

But what about Shi Hua, Luc, and everyone else back at the Crimson Palace? Turn the page for a preview of *A Hint of Thief!*

A Hint of Thief

Lady Shi Hua of Jing suppressed a shiver as she disembarked the *Unbridled*. It would not do for the wife of the soon-to-be crowned emperor of Jing to show any emotion. Her fellow citizens waiting to greet their new ruler examined her for any possible weakness. Any little tidbit they could use against her, or worse Po.

Curiosity slammed against her mental shields. Both Reverend Father Jin and Brother Jian fed their energy into her to reinforce her power. For a brief instant, she missed Brother Jeremy of Issura. They'd fought demons and conceived a child together, but there was a sweetness to him that had been reassuring, and she'd shared far more of herself with him than she did with her friends here in Jing. If she desired men, maybe she would have stayed in Issura.

But Po needed someone to watch his back all day, everyday. The only person who could do that would be the empress. It wasn't a role she desired, but her Temple training emphasized duty. Being his wife and the new empress of Jing meant fulfilling her duty of protecting humanity by keeping the Jing Empire politically stable in order to battle the latest demon incursions.

Warden Mateqai's presence at her back eased some of her tension. She'd come to depend on him during her time with the Issuran Temple of Light. As much as she wanted him to stay with her as part of her personal guard, she couldn't ask him to abandon his people, his culture, his position for a post in a foreign country half a world away from his home.

At the end of the gangplank, the Imperial Guard stood at attention. The twin lines ended with Duke Bao Lixin of Huang He and his retinue. The duke was one of the many distant cousins who could possibly claim the throne should something happen to Po. However, both Reverend Father Jin of Light and Reverend Father Biming of Thief assured Po of this particular cousin's loyalty.

Shi Hua prayed they had actually truthspelled the duke and asked a justice to perform the interrogation. As she learned while serving in Issura, a good justice was needed to make sure the right questions were asked.

She studied the duke while she and her husband strode down the ceremonial line. He stood approximately two handspans taller than herself, but a handspan shorter than Po. The duke carried the sharp cheekbones and dimpled chin of the Bao linage, but his wide shoulders and bowlegged stance showed traits of the nobility in Huang He.

They reached the duke, who executed a proper bow. "The new emperor honors me and my people with his presence."

Before Po could respond, a flash of movement to her left caught her attention. A citizen dressed as a guard raised something to his mouth.

Instinct kicked into motion. Shi Hua knocked Po to the carpet-covered ground, covered him with her body, and raised wards around them. An Imperial guardsman collapsed next to the pair, a dart stabbing his cheek. The guardsman convulsed.

Chaos and screaming erupted around them. Warden Mateqai, Captain Huizhong, and the rest of the guards closed ranks to protect Po, but not before Brother Fa raced past them in his white tiger form.

From underneath Shi Hua, Po whispered, "For once, could you save my life without landing on top of me?"

Glossary
Words and Phrases Specific to the Justice Series

Anacapa Islands – a series of four islands off the southwestern coast of Issura. Limuw is the largest. Wi'ma is the second largest. Anacapa is the closest to Orrin. Tuqan is the furthest from Orrin.

Apprentice – lowest rank of a trade or craft guild

Berda – gender fluid; someone who does not stick to traditional gender roles

Britannia – Toscan name for a series of islands off the western coast of the Old Continent. The two largest are Eire and Albion. Four hundred years before Anthea's time, the queens of Eire and Albion were losing their battle against the demons. They ordered the islands evacuated and the Temples of Death to launch their last resort spells. The islands are now barren, and no one who steps on them lives for long.

Briton Diaspora – refers to the survivors and their descendants of the evacuation of Britannia who are now scattered around the world

Brother – title for any fully ordained priest of any Temple that accepts men, except for the Temple of Father

Cant – Issura's neighboring nation-state to the south

Chengzhou – the capital of Jing, a nation-state in the western shore of the Old Continent

Chief Justice – title of the highest ranked priestess at a Temple of Balance

Chief [name of trade] – the highest ranking master guild member of a trade in a city or region

The Cradle – according to legend, the continent where Child created the first members of the human race

Duke/Duchess – highest ranking noble of a region

Distance-view glasses – a telescope

Father – title for any fully ordained priest of the Temple of Father

Gilwas – a city in northern Issura

Gray Mountains – a mountain range that runs the entire length of the western side of the Long Continents

The Grand Canal – a human-built canal that passes through the isthmus connecting the Long Continents

The Great Forest – the rainforest that covers nearly half of the Southern Long Continent on the north side

The Green Lady Inn – an inn near the Embassy District of Orrin, it has the only entrance/exit to the tunnel system with the city wall that is not a Temple

Guild – a civil organization for a trade or craft

Guild Master – an expert tradesman's rank based on analysis of his/her peers

Healer – a person with the magical ability to heal illness and repair wounds

High Brother – title of the chief priest of a city Temple, except the Temple of Father

High Father – title of the chief priest of a city's Temple of Father

High Mother – title of the chief priestess of a city's Temple of Mother

High Sister – title of the chief priestess of a city Temple, except the Temples of Balance or Mother

Iberia – nation-state on the southwestern corner of the Old Continent

Issura – queendom on the western coast of Northern Long Continent; the Peaceful Sea forms its western border with the nation of Pagonia to the north, the nation of Cant to the south, the nations of the Cliffdwellers and Diné to the southeast and the Gray Mountains to the east

Jing – nation-state on the eastern side of the Old Continent

Journeyman/Journeywoman – middle rank of a trade or craft guild

Justice – title for any fully ordained priestess of the Temple of Balance; alternate term of address is Lady Justice

Kemet – nation-state on the northeast corner of the Cradle

Kulshra'jek Pass – a pass through the Gray Mountains adjacent to Pana Valley, mainly used by Comanche traders in the summer on their way west

Lake Tulamniu – a lake at the south end of Pana Valley

The Levant – a loose alliance of Phoenician city-states between the Hittite Empire and Kemet on the eastern side of the Middle Sea

The Long Continents – the two continents separating the Peaceful Sea from the Panthalassa Sea, they are connected by a narrow isthmus

The Lost Continent – southern continent between the Peaceful Sea and the Storm Sea. By Anthea's time, the original inhabitants were believed to be slaughtered by demons 500 years before. Sailors from the Sea Peoples and Maurya who landed there after the inhabitants' disappearance reported screams but found no one. Those with magic talents went mad. Not even the priests and priestesses from Child could save them. Those who tried went mad themselves.

Magistrate – elected official of a city or town in Issura who is responsible for civil and criminal law enforcement and the city or town's defense/care in an emergency

Master – senior member of a trade or craft guild; the clergyperson who is primarily responsible for the training of a novice class

Maurya – the southern-most nation of the Old Continent

Middle Sea – shallow sea that separate The Cradle from the Old Continent

Mother – title for any fully ordained priestess of the Temple of Father

Naha – capital of the Kingdom of Ryukyu, a set of islands in the Peaceful Sea southwest of the Fire Islands

National Road – main, paved road through the nation of Issura. It roughly parallels the western coastline.

New Thenos – an island city/state on the eastern coast of the Northern Long Continent

Novice – a person in training to become a priest/priestess of the Twelve

Orrin – third largest city in the queendom of Issura with the second largest port

Pagonia – Issura's neighboring nation to the north

Panthalassa Sea – ocean that separates the Long Continents from the western part of the Old Continent and the Cradle

Peaceful Sea – ocean that separates the Long Continents from the eastern part of the Old Continent, the islands and archipelagos of the Sea Peoples, and the Lost Continent

Peacekeepers – men and women who act as a city's police force. They report to the city's magistrate. They also act as an auxiliary defense force if their city or nation is attacked.

Pimu – one of a series of four islands off the northern coast of Cant

Rambla – a city in northern Cant, its people were used to hatch demon eggs off-screen during the events of *A Modicum of Truth*

Redwood Grove – a fair-sized town in the northeastern section of the Duchy of Orrin. It nestles on a plateau in the foothills of the Grey Mountains near the border with the Duchy of Pana.

Reverend Father – senior-most priest of a Temple order, the leader of that sect in the nation in which he resides

Reverend Mother – senior-most priestess of a Temple order, the leader of that sect in the nation in which she resides

Ryukyu – a kingdom consisting of a set of islands in the Peaceful Sea southwest of the Fire Islands

Seat – person holding the highest ranking position of a Temple

Shakya – nation-state in the western portion of the Old Continent, southwest of Jing and northeast of Maurya

Sister – title for any fully ordained priestess of any Temple that accepts women, except for the Temples of Mother and Balance

Skinwalker – a human with talent who performs demon magic; the magic corrupts their physical body to the point they need another person's skin to contain their spirit

Standora – capital and largest city of Issura

Storm Sea – ocean bordered by the eastern part of the Cradle, the southern part of the Old Continent, and the western part of the Lost Continent

Tandor – Issuran city that guards the border with Cant and Diné

Temple – a collection of people dedicated to the service of one of the twelve gods; a building that houses such people; the primary place of worship for one of the twelve gods

Tiwan – the capital of Cant

Toscana – nation-state on the southwest section of the Old Continent; location of the first battle against the demons

Tupi – one of the indigenous tribes of the Great Forest, they are known for their Vintner's variety of medicinal plants

The Twelve – the collective name for the twelve deities of the Justice universe

Valencia – duchy in the nation-state of Iberia; know for their innovative shipbuilding designs

Valley of the Lost – the desert between Issura, Diné, and the Cliffdweller Territory

Warden – security guard of a Temple, they act as supplementary military personnel in the event of a demon invasion

Wechuge – a human who commits the sin of cannibalism, they are transformed into a creature of ice and magic

The Twelve Temples

Mother

Cloak Color – Light blue

Motto – "To give without thought; to forgive with love."

The Temple of Mother is responsible for the teaching of household arts, such as spinning, weaving, food storage and preparation. The order is also responsible for caring for those who have lost their families.

Father

Cloak Color – Dark blue

Motto – "All tools are weapons, and weapons tools."

The Temple of Father is responsible for the constructive arts, such as carpentry and smithing.

Balance

Cloak Color – Black

Motto – "Balance in all things."

The Temple of Balance runs the judicial system. A justice is the judge in criminal and civil cases.

Light

Cloak Color – Medium brown

Motto – "Light brings truth, for without truth, there can be no justice."

The Temple of Light is responsible for codifying contracts and mediating contract disputes. A Light priest also acts as the bailiff for a justice, and is often the one to truthspell a witness or the accused. The Temple of Light also provides military support to a nation's civilian army.

Knowledge

Cloak Color – Gold

Motto – "With patience, knowledge comes."

The Temple of Knowledge is responsible for education and for recording historical events. They essentially act as the library system for the Justice universe.

Thief

Cloak Color – Grey

Motto – "Hiding in plain sight."

The Temple of Thief acts as the intelligence-gathering arm of both the Temples and the civilian leaders. They finance their efforts through gambling dens.

Conflict

Cloak Color – Dark Red

Motto – "Destruction is the necessary evil, for it clears the way for new growth."

The Temple of Conflict focuses on strategy and all martial arts. They are the primary support and teachers of a nation's army.

Love

Cloak Color – Medium Red

Motto – "Pleasure is life."

The Temple of Love are the holy prostitutes. They also deal with sex education and lead the Spring Rituals, the annual fertility rites which were first used to breed as many humans with magical talent as possible. Don't underestimate them. They fight just as hard and as nasty as their fellow clergy in Conflict.

Child

Cloak Color – Light green

Motto – "All things are new once."

The Temple of Child is responsible for the emotional health of citizens. They also develop and teach agriculture and animal husbandry techniques.

Wilding

Cloak Color – Dark green

Motto – "All creatures return to us."

The Temple of the Wildling God deals with management of wild animal populations, forestry, and the protection of ecosystems.

Vintner

Cloak Color – Purple

Motto – "The line between wisdom and madness is one sip."

The Temple of Vintner not only deals with the cultivation of grapes and the production of wine, but they also promote the gathering, cultivation and processing of all medicinal herbs.

Death

Cloak Color – Black

Motto – "For every life, there is a death."

The Temple of Death takes care of the gathering of the dead, the last rites, and disposal of the corpses. They also act as a repository for the last wills and testaments of all citizens.

Characters and Places

QUEENDOM OF ISURRA

ORRIN

Temple of Balance

Chief Justice Anthea – a circuit justice for ten winters until her appointment as Chief Justice of Orrin at the age of thirty winters ("Justice")

Chief Justice Penelope – deceased, predecessor to Anthea as Chief Justice of Orrin

Chief Justice Thalia – deceased, predecessor to Penelope as Chief Justice of Orrin, maternal grandmother to Anthea

Justice Yanaba – junior justice assigned to the city of Orrin after the events of *A Question of Balance*

Justice Erato – junior justice assigned to the circuit of the eastern section of the duchy of Orrin and the southern tip of the duchy of Pana Valley after Anthea is sentenced to the seat of Orrin in "Justice"

Sivan – personal assistant to Chief Justice Anthea and head of the household staff

Donella – senior clerk

Lailani – junior clerk

Chief Warden Little Bear – head of the Balance wardens

Warden Tyra – junior warden, killed in the Battle of Tandor (*A Matter of Death*)

Warden Gina – junior warden

Warden Aglaia – junior warden, died in the battle to retake the Temple of Love (*A Question of Balance*)

Warden Daniel – junior warden

Warden Noko – junior warden

Warden Jonata – junior warden, Aglaia's replacement from the Standora Wardens' Academy, a passive talent

Warden Dezba – junior warden

Warden Tahoma – junior warden

Warden Ahiga – junior warden

Warden Long Feather – junior warden

Warden Ailyn – junior warden, she replaced Tyra after her death

Warden Mylon – junior warden

Hogarth – former chief warden under Justices Thalia and Penelope, now stablemaster, husband of Deborah

Deborah – Head cook, wife of Hogarth

Nathan – squire to Chief Justice Anthea after he was sentenced to pay reparations for stealing bread, an orphan, age ten winters at the time of his sentencing in *A Question of Balance*

Ming Wei – squire to Justice Yanaba, nine winters old at the end of *A Question of Balance*. Originally from Jing, she was sold by her parents to a Jing noble as a sex slave and brought to Issura. When the noble's crimes were discovered, he immolated himself and his slaves. Ming Wei was the only survivor and has severe scar tissue on her face, back and arms.

Kosumi – the son of Justice Yanaba and High Brother Xander, conceived due to the breeding edict issued worldwide by the Reverend Mothers of Justice and the Reverend Fathers of Light, born between the events of *A Hand of Father* and *A Measure of Knowledge*

Temple of Light

High Brother Luc – a circuit priest for twelve winters until his appointment as chief priest at the age of thirty-two winters between the events of "Justice" and "Diplomacy in the Dark"

High Brother Kam – semi-retired, predecessor to Luc as chief priest, poisoned and died during the events of *A Question of Balance*

Brother Mat – Second to Luc. His birth name is Micah. He murdered the real Mat on his way to Orrin from Standora. Died under Anthea's truthspell interrogation in *A Question of Balance*.

Brother Jeremy – youngest junior priest until he is promoted to Luc's second after the events of *A Question of Balance*.

Brother Garbhan – junior priest who is assigned permanently to Orrin after the events of *A Matter of Death*

Brother Wolf Run – junior priest partnered with Justice Erato on the eastern Orrin circuit

Istaqa – personal assistant to High Brother Luc and head of the household staff

Edberth – former personal assistant to High Brother Kam, he now acts as evening assistant to High Brother Luc

Henry – stablemaster

Chief Warden Nicholas – head of the Light wardens

Warden Gibb – junior warden, died shortly after the renegades' kidnapping of High Brother Luc in *A Question of Balance*

Warden Mateqai – junior warden, becomes Sister Shi Hua's personal bodyguard during the events of *A Modicum of Truth*

Warden Yar – junior warden

Warden Tadhg – junior warden

Warden Gad – junior warden

Chao – the son of Sister Shi Hua and Brother Jeremy, conceived due to the breeding edict issued worldwide by the Reverend Mothers of Justice and the Reverend Fathers of Light, born between the events of *A Hand of Father* and *A Measure of Knowledge*

Temple of Love

High Sister Gerd – chief priestess, biological daughter of Thalia and Kam, biological mother of Anthea. She was removed from office on charges of fraud, bribery of a public official, unlawful magic, and conspiracy to commit murder. Later, the charges of dealing in demon artifacts and treason were added.

Sister Dragonfly – Gerd's second, *berda* (genderfluid), is acting High Sister after the events in *A Question of Balance*, becomes High Sister after the events in *A Modicum of Truth*

Sister Gretchen – junior priestess, deceased. The discovery of her body in one of Duke Marco's wine barrels precipitates the events in *A Question of Balance*.

Sister Claudia – junior priestess, Dragonfly's second

Sister Shada – junior priestess

Sister Zihna – junior priestess

Sister Ilina – Gerd's second until her death; Lady Katarina DiMara's mother; she died of the wasting disease a year prior to "Justice"

Chief Warden Citana – new chief warden of Love after renegades killed and replaced the entire warden contingent of the temple

Warden Jocasta – junior warden, one of the replacement wardens after the events of *A Question of Balance*

Warden Ekta – junior warden

Gregorios – a eunuch who was High Sister Dragonfly's personal assistant and head of household until their murder prior to the beginning of *A Twist of Love*

Ichik – a eunuch who is Sister Claudia's personal assistant

Iona – Love's maintenance person, she does minor repairs and servicing of the Temple

Temple of Conflict

High Brother Han – chief priest

Brother Piru – junior priest, Han's second

Sister Migina – junior priestess

Brother Yas – junior priest

Brother Keanu – junior priest

Temple of Death

High Sister Bertrice – chief priestess

High Brother Kai – deceased, predecessor of Bertrice, retired in Bertrice's favor as the temple seat and became a teaching brother in Standora until his death

Brother Xander – Bertrice's second until her demise during the Battle of Tandor, succeeds her as Orrin's High Brother of Death

Sister Raven Claw – Xander's second when he becomes high brother

Brother Elu – junior priest

Chief Warden Axton – head of the Death wardens

Warden Hitari – junior warden

Temple of Vintner

High Brother Ben – chief priest

Sister Nina – junior priestess

Chief Warden Mangas – head of the Vintner wardens

Warden Golden Eagle – junior warden, murdered by Gerd during the events of *A Twist of Love*

Temple of Mother

High Mother Bianca – chief priestess, she commits suicide when Anthea discovers Bianca has been selling children

High Mother Leocadia – chief priestess, she transferred from the Temple in Gilwas and succeeded Bianca between the events in *A Touch of Mother* and *A Twist of Love*

Chief Warden Maebh – head of the Mother wardens until the events of *A Touch of Mother*

Ademaro – Leocadia's personal chef she brought with her from Gilwas

Temple of Father

High Father Jerrod – chief priest

Temple of Child

High Sister Mya – chief priestess

Brother Turtle – junior priest, helps to save Justice Yanaba by pulling her soul back into her body during the events of *A Modicum of Truth*

Sister Dawn Star – junior priestess

Makawee – Child's head of household and Mya's personal assistant

Chief Warden High Rock – head of the Child wardens

Temple of Wildling

High Brother Jax – chief priest, second form is a wolf

Sister Farrah – Jax's second, second form is a fox

Temple of Thief

High Brother Talbert – chief priest

Sister Cedar Grove – Talbert's second

Brother Teluhci – junior priest

Sister Malila – junior priestess

Chief Warden Sabine – head of the Thief wardens

Temple of Knowledge

High Sister Mariana – chief priestess

Brother Luca – junior priest

Nobility

Duke Benedetto DiMara – father of Marco, Alessa, and Isabella, husband of Cora, convicted of conspiracy to use illegal magic to mind wipe his son Marco during the events of "Justice"; imprisoned at Standora for life.

Lady Cora DiMara – mother of Marco, Alessa, and Isabella, convicted of treason and demon dealing, executed by the Reverend Mother Alara of Balance during the events of "Justice".

Duke Marco DiMara – duke of Orrin, inherited his post at the age of eighteen winters after his parents were found guilty of numerous offenses and stripped of their titles and property

Lady Katarina DiMara (nee' DiLove) – common-born wife of Marco, animal healer. Her mother was Sister Ilina, a priestess of the Temple of Love who died of the wasting sickness the summer before Katarina's eighteenth winter.

Lord Kam DiMara – eldest child of Marco and Katarina and heir to the Duchy of Orrin, named for High Brother Kam of Light, godson of Chief Justice Anthea and High Brother Luc

Lady Alessa DiMara – sister of Marco, a passive talent, lover of Sister Gretchen of Love

Lady Isabella DiMara – sister of Marco, attends the University of Standora

Bartholomew – retainer of Duke Marco's until it was learned he'd assaulted Lady Alessa and Sister Gretchen. Lady Alessa subsequently asked Chief Justice Anthea for clemency and hired him to manage the estates Sister Gretchen had bequeathed to Alessa.

William – retainer of Duke Marco's

Julian – retainer of Duke Marco's

Noemi – a handmaid to Lady Alessa

Arturo – former captain of Duke Marco's flagship. His murder is the precipitating event of "Diplomacy in the Dark".

Titus – captain of Duke Marco's flagship, the *Mars Tranquilus*

Lady Aurora – a noblewoman who commissioned a ceremonial silver knife as a gift to her groom from Govind, Anthea confiscated the knife in order to kill a wechuge

Citizens

Malven DiCook – duly elected magistrate of Orrin

Dante – one of Orrin's peacekeepers, dies at the beginning of *A Modicum of Truth*

Barbora – wife of Dante, dies at the beginning of *A Modicum of Truth*

Jaime – one of Orrin's peacekeepers

Leyti – one of Orrin's peacekeepers

Fat Squirrel – one of Orrin's peacekeepers

Drest – a peacekeeper, dismissed by DiCook for extortion

Robin – a peacekeeper, dismissed by DiCook for warning Drest that DiCook was coming to arrest him

Alo – an innkeeper, the owner of the Green Lady Inn near the Embassy District

Xoco – Alo's wife who died giving birth to Chumana

Chumana – Alo's daughter, she is ten winters at the beginning of *A Question of Balance*

Cat and Dog – the leaders of Orrin's street children, Chief Justice Anthea uses them to obtain information outside of the normal Temple intelligence channels

Harold – an Orrin wagoneer

Chief Healer Aaron – head of the Healers' Guild

Master Healer Devin – second to Aaron in the Orrin Healer's Guild, originally from New Thenos

Journeywoman Bly – a junior healer, often assists Master Devin at autopsies, later a master healer in her own right

Simi – Bly's apprentice at the Healers Guild when Bly attains master status

Master Healer Una – a master healer who specializes in head trauma and sleep disorders, she also happens to be a dreamwalker

EAGLE REACH

Kele – a farmer outside of the village, Hania's brother

Pavati – Kele's daughter who went missing on her way to Redwood Grove before the events of *A Virtue of Child*

REDWOOD GROVE

Hania – a farmer outside of the town, Kele's brother

TANDOR

High Brother Dav – chief priest of the Temple of Light

Chief Justice Elizabeth – chief justice of the Temple of Balance

Minerva – the new clerk with the Temple of Balance, a renegade, killed during the fight within the Temple of Balance (*A Modicum of Truth*)

High Brother Aduba – chief priest of the Temple of Conflict

Brother Tighan – second of the Temple of Conflict, a renegade, killed by Aduba during the fall of Tandor

High Brother Nantan – chief priest of the Temple of Death

Sister Reby – second of the Temple of the Wildling God, first introduced as a shapeshifting thief in "The Perfect Partner", second form is a polecat

Brother Sisquoc – priest of the Temple of the Wildling God, second form is a panther

Brother Trajan – priest of the Temple of the Wilding God, second form is a wolf

Sister Jumping Mouse – priestess of the Temple of the Wildling God, second form is a kangaroo rat

Duke Enzo DiToscana – Duke of Tandor, murdered by a skinwalker possessing his wife

Duchess Nadine DiToscana – the widow of Duke Enzo of Tandor

Ural DiSand – merchant from Tandor, implicated in the Assassin Guild plots in Orrin, killed while possessed by a skinwalker (*A Modicum of Truth*)

Amarantha DiRoma – Tandoran merchant, rival of Ural DiSand, murdered by renegades shortly before they poisoned most of the personnel of the Tandoran Temples

Govind – a silversmith who assisted with the defense of Tandor against the demon army, settled in Orrin after the evacuation and fall of Tandor

The Wave Dancer – Duchess Nadine of Tandor's flagship, one of two remaining ships in Tandor prior to the Battle of Tandor

STANDORA – capital city of Issura

Reverend Mother Alara – head of Issura's Temple of Balance

Justice Rose – novice training priestess of the main Temple of Balance in Standora when Anthea was a novice

Justice Melanippe – a novice in Anthea's class. She was the top student, but she was also recruited by Thief to report on any wrongdoing in Balance.

Reverend Father Farrell – head of Issura's Temple of Light

Brother Elroy – a Light priest, aide to Reverend Father Farrell, and a distance speaker who accompanies the Isurran and Sea Peoples fleets to Tandor in *A Matter of Death*

Brother Long Wind – a Light priest and aide to Reverend Father Farrell; he accompanies the queen's army to Tandor in *A Matter of Death*

Brother Garbhan – a Light priest and aide to Reverend Father Farrell; he remains in Orrin during and after the events of *A Matter of Death*

Brother Jon – novice training priest at the main Temple of Light in Standora, murdered by the skinwalker at Samael DiRoy's abandoned manse prior to *A Question of Balance*

Brother Gáagii – a junior Light priest

Reverend Mother Sxa'min – head of Issura's Temple of Love

High Sister Imala – a Love priestess, considered to be the lead contender for position of Reverend Mother of Love; she accompanies the queen's army in A Matter of Death

Chief Warden Catherine – Imala's chief warden; she was a classmate of Mateqai's at the Warden Academy and the two had a physical relationship

Warden Hototo – a junior Love warden

Reverend Father Grey Shadow – head of Issura's Temple of Thief

Brother White Wolf – a senior priest of Thief; he's a personal friend of High Sister Imala

Queen Teodora – reigning monarch of Issura

Crown Princess Chiara – eldest child and heir of Queen Teodora of Issura; lady general of the queen's army

Duke White Eagle – former Conflict brother, left the order to marry Crown Princess Chiara; honorary title Duke of Standora as the future queen's consort; lord general of the queen's army

PANA VALLEY

Lord Aleister DeGrove – noble noted for his vineyards

JING EMPIRE

CHENGZHOU

Empress Bao De – ruler of Jing a century before Bao Yu, she sacrificed herself to stop a demon army

Empress Bao Yu – ruler of Jing until her death from natural causes during "Courting Trouble"

Emperor Bao Chengwu – current ruler of Jing, succeeded his mother Bao Yu during "Courting Trouble"

Ambassador Quan Po – half-brother of the current Jing emperor Bao Chengwu; was heir to the throne until his nephew was born

Reverend Father Jin – head of Jing's Temple of Light

Sister Shi Hua – a priestess of Light, who was tapped as Po's bodyguard. She received additional training from Conflict, Thief, and Love. Originally from the town of Yintze in the southern province of Chu.

Brother Lin – novice master of Light

Brother Jian – a priest of Light, classmate of Shi Hua during their novice years

Brother Fa – a Wildling priest, his second form is a tiger, a friend of Shi Hua and Jian during their novice years

Justice Mei Wen – a priestess of Balance, Shi Hua's closest friend other than Jian during their novice years

Sister Yin Li – a priestess of Love, Shi Hua's maternal aunt

Yin Shang – the son of Sister Yin Li and Brother Shang

Reverend Father Chen – head of Jing's Temple of Conflict

Reverend Father Feng – replaced Chen after the disappearance of him and his army before A Touch of Mother

Brother Shang – a priest of Conflict, Shi Hua's instructor when she was a novice

Reverend Father Biming – head of Jing's Temple of Thief

The Unbridled – a spy ship used by the Temple of Thief, a four-masted carrack built in the Iberian duchy of Valencia, captained by Reverend Father Biming during *A Modicum of Truth*

Brother Hadar – a priest of Thief from the Kingdom of Hejaz, serving on board *The Unbridled*

Kingdom of O'ahu

Prince Alika – youngest son of the king of the Sea Peoples, one of Sister Gretchen's worshippers, the father of her unborn child

Captain Iakepa – senior captain of the O'ahu trading fleet

DINÉ NATION

AJÉÍ (HEART)

Temple of Balance

Reverend Mother Hózhó – head of the Diné Temple of Balance

Justice Mosi – a junior justice

Justice Spotted Fawn – the western circuit justice for the Diné Nation, killed in the Battle of Tandor

Bidzii – Spotted Fawn's clerk, he was fluent in Issuran so the justice spoke through him; killed in the Battle of Tandor

Temple of Light

Brother Bumblebee – junior priest of Light with the Diné army, Anthea's half-brother by her father Kilchii

Temple of Conflict

Reverend Father Kilchii – head of the Diné Temple of Conflict. When he first met Anthea, he gave his name as "Nizhé'é'", which in the Diné language means "your father" because he is her biological father.

Temple of Knowledge

Sister Lizard – junior priestess with the Diné army at Tandor

Temple of Thief

Sister Shideezhi – junior priestess, Anthea's half-sister by their father Kilchii

Temple of Wildling

Sister Cheona – junior priestess, her second form is a panther

Elders

Matriarch Nascha – elected leader of the Diné Nation, a clan elder

Elder Johona – a clan elder

Elder Chooli – a clan elder who was murdered to fuel the hatching of a demon egg

Niyol – Nacha's eldest brother

Sike – Johona's eldest brother

Tibah – deceased, Chief Justice Thalia's mother, Reverend Mother Hózhó and Matriarch Nascha's great-aunt, and Chief Justice Anthea's great-grandmother

CLIFFDWELLERS

Healer Kotori – a physician with the Diné army during the siege of Tandor

PLAINS NATIONS – COMANCHE

High Brother Pecos – a senior Conflict priest with the Diné army during the siege of Tandor

THE KINGDOM OF RYUKYU

NAHA

Temple of Thief

Reverend Father Ogusuku – head of the Ryukyu Temple of Thief

Sister Jade – junior priestess, assigned as Anthea and Shi Hua's bodyguard while they were in Ryukyu

Sister Jasmine – junior priestess, assigned as Anthea and Shi Hua's bodyguard while they were in Ryukyu

ACKNOWLEDGMENTS

Thank you to Elaina Lee and Jaye Manus for making my books look their best, inside and out.

Much love to my husband and my writing partner, Bella the Princess Pup.

And most of all, thank you to all of you readers who've taken the Justice universe into your hearts.

Suzan Harden transitioned from writing information technology manuals for companies and legal articles for a law enforcement magazine to her first love, fantasy and science fiction in all their forms. She's the author of the Bloodlines, the 888-555-HERO, and the Justice series.

www.ingramcontent.com/pod-product-compliance
Lightning Source LLC
Chambersburg PA
CBHW070532100726
47907CB00004B/1092